Antonio Tenderly Touched Her Face With A Fingertip. "Do You Remember What You Asked Of Me Before You Fell Asleep, Maria?"

She did. Vividly. *Show me what I need to know about love.*

And, strangely enough, the only thing that had changed was her confidence that she could handle the lessons she'd requested of him.

"I remember," she said, watching his expression. "I'd still like you to show me. I'm just not sure how."

He observed her for a long time before answering. "It's up to the man to know how. It's up to you, the woman, only to say yes or no."

A rush of heat swept through her body. When she tried to speak, the words dried up before crossing her lips. At last she managed the only ones that seemed important. "Then I say yes."

Dear Reader,

In honor of International Women's Day, March 8, celebrate romance, love and the accomplishments of women all over the world by reading six passionate, powerful and provocative new titles from Silhouette Desire.

New York Times bestselling author Sharon Sala leads the Desire lineup with *Amber by Night* (#1495). A shy librarian uses her alter ego to win her lover's heart in a sizzling love story by this beloved MIRA and Intimate Moments author. Next, a pretend affair turns to true passion when a Barone heroine takes on the competition, in *Sleeping with Her Rival* (#1496) by Sheri WhiteFeather, the third title of the compelling DYNASTIES: THE BARONES saga.

A single mom shares a heated kiss with a stranger on New Year's Eve and soon after reencounters him at work, in *Renegade Millionaire* (1497) by Kristi Gold. *Mail-Order Prince in Her Bed* (#1498) by Kathryn Jensen features an Italian nobleman who teaches an American ingenue the language of love, while a city girl and a rancher get together with the help of her elderly aunt, in *The Cowboy Claims His Lady* (#1499) by Meagan McKinney, the latest MATCHED IN MONTANA title. And a contractor searching for his secret son finds love in the arms of the boy's adoptive mother, in *Tangled Sheets, Tangled Lies* (#1500) by brand-new author Julie Hogan, debuting in the Desire line.

Delight in all six of these sexy Silhouette Desire titles this month…and every month.

Enjoy!

Joan Marlow Golan

Joan Marlow Golan
Senior Editor, Silhouette Desire

Please address questions and book requests to:
Silhouette Reader Service
U.S.: 3010 Walden Ave., P.O. Box 1325, Buffalo, NY 14269
Canadian: P.O. Box 609, Fort Erie, Ont. L2A 5X3

Mail-Order Prince in Her Bed

KATHRYN JENSEN

Silhouette®

Desire®

Published by Silhouette Books

America's Publisher of Contemporary Romance

SILHOUETTE BOOKS

ISBN 0-373-76498-7

MAIL-ORDER PRINCE IN HER BED

Visit Silhouette at www.eHarlequin.com

Printed in U.S.A.

Books by Kathryn Jensen

Silhouette Desire

I Married a Prince #1115
The Earl Takes a Bride #1282
Mail-Order Cinderella #1318
The Earl's Secret #1343
The American Earl #1347
The Secret Prince #1428
The Royal & the Runaway Bride #1448
Mail-Order Prince in Her Bed #1498

Silhouette Intimate Moments

Time and Again #685
Angel's Child #758
The Twelve-Month Marriage #797

KATHRYN JENSEN

has written over forty novels for adults and children,
under various names, and lived in many interesting
places, including Texas, Connecticut and Italy. She cur-
rently resides in Maryland with her husband and two
feline writing companions, Miranda and Tempest, who
behave precisely as their names indicate—the first,
sweetly...the second, mischievously. Their thirty-two-
foot sailboat, *Purr,* promises to carry all four on many
new adventures. Aboard her is where Kathryn does
much of her summer writing.

For Roger, with all my heart:

Two souls, unaware,
felt the Italian sun.
Now sail love's fair seas
on the *S. V. Purr.*

One

The situation was far worse than he'd imagined. Antonio Boniface stepped off the elevator at the tenth floor of the Washington, D.C., high-rise and stared at the plaque on the heavy oak door facing him—Klein & Klein Public Relations and Advertising. Quickly, he checked the address on the slip of paper, his eyes narrowing, the muscles across his stomach clenching as if in preparation for an opponent's punch. Marco had said nothing about the place being a business establishment. He'd assumed he would end up at the woman's apartment.

Don't make more of this than necessary, he told himself firmly. A simple explanation to this Maria McPherson, the client Marco had been on his way to see before Antonio and U.S. Immigration had caught up with him. That was all that was required.

"Scusi, signorina—" No! English, he corrected himself, speak in English! "Pardon me, miss. Mr. Serilo is no longer employed by the Royal Escort Service. If you tell me how

much you paid for his services, I shall be happy to reimburse you."

There. What was so difficult about that? For one thing, he hadn't counted on approaching the woman at her workplace with such delicate news.

But too much was at stake to back down now. He couldn't let Marco's use of his family's illustrious name bring further dishonor. The Bonifaces d'Apulia had once ranked alongside the Medicis in power, had been benefactors to great artists including Michelangelo and Leonardo da Vinci. Their aristocratic roots extended back to the twelfth century, included two popes, illustrious statesmen, men and women of vision and pride. No rogue servant would be allowed to tarnish that name while Antonio lived!

Determined, he turned the knob and pushed through the door, into a gray-and-beige reception area furnished in sterile Scandinavian decor. The receptionist's desk was vacant. No one seemed to be around. What to do now?

Suddenly, he heard shouts burst out from behind a half-closed door to his right. Antonio swung around, strode toward it with purpose, peered through the crack.

The conference room was jammed with men and women in business attire. On a long mahogany table at the room's center was a neon-frosted cake, candles ablaze. Poised over the cake, her cheeks puffed out in preparation for extinguishing a blinding array of candles, was a petite young woman with cool gray eyes and long, wavy hair the color of champagne. She delicately blew out each candle then straightened and smiled nervously at the crowd around her.

"There. Now everybody enjoy a piece of cake. I really do have to get back to work," she said, starting to turn away.

"Whoa! Not so fast, Maria." A tall woman with blunt-cut black hair laughed, stepping forward to block her path. "Your present hasn't arrived yet."

A titter went up around the room, and Antonio guessed that everyone knew what that gift was to be.

Marco.

Clearly, the woman whose birthday they were celebrating did not.

He observed the waiflike creature, feeling sorry for her. Sensing also, in a sudden, too-vague recollection, that he had seen those gentle features before. Somewhere. The sense of familiarity was haunting, gnawed at his mind. But both place and time ultimately eluded him.

Maria shook her head nervously. "Please, Tamara, you shouldn't go to all this trouble for me."

"Oh, it's *our* pleasure, dear. I think we'll get as much out of this gift as you will."

"Not if she's lucky!" a voice rang out from the crowd, and everyone broke into laughter.

So that was their plan, Antonio thought. These sophisticated, brash PR types had decided to have a little fun at the expense of their bashful co-worker. They had sent for a mail-order prince as offered in the escort service's vulgar advertisement.

Fortunately, his good friend the Senator had seen it and sent him a copy. The knave had been using Antonio's name and official title, *Il Principe di Carovigno,* as his own. At least the service hadn't been bold enough to use a photograph too!

In a way, it was a lucky thing for Miss McPherson that he'd learned of his former employee's deception and sent the Casanova packing. The young woman he was watching tentatively nibble a slice of the gaudy cake wouldn't have to suffer the indignities of Marco's foolish performance, whatever that might entail. For all Antonio knew it might have involved removing articles of clothing. Or worse!

But would his walking in and announcing that the game was over only delay the young woman's torment? A new scheme might soon replace the original farce. His heart went out to her. If there was any way of saving her further embarrassment…

The solution came to him in an unexpected flash of inspiration.

Antonio pushed through the door and into the conference room. All talk ceased. He smiled around the room at the women, fixed the male employees with a daunting glare, then turned his darkest, most mysterious gaze on the birthday girl.

"Ah, *signorina*," he said, bowing as he approached. He lifted her limp fingertips to his lips. "It is a pleasure to finally meet you. I've heard so much about you, *cara mia*." Yes, he was laying the accent on a bit thick, but he suspected that would have been Marco's style.

A worried smile hovered over Maria's lips. She blinked up at him, at a loss. "Y-you have?"

"*Sì.* Your friends have arranged for you to share *l'avventura* with me. I believe you have the rest of the day off?" The raven-haired woman nodded, her eyes wide, appreciative and more than a little envious. "*Andiamo, cara.* My car waits for us."

Maria shot a panicky glance around the room, then looked pleadingly at Antonio as she sidled closer to him. "You don't have to do this," she whispered. "I know it's all a joke."

"But Signorina McPherson, it is my pleasure," he said aloud, giving her a conspiratorial wink. He placed a hand at the hollow of her slim back and guided her firmly toward the door. She wore a conservative sweaterlike dress of a synthetic fiber—black, a bit scratchy to the touch.

He imagined her in cashmere, perhaps a soft blue to set off her eyes. Much better.

Tamara finally found her feet and rushed to catch up with them. She handed Maria her purse, coat and a card. "Have fun, honey. This will explain the services your date is prepared to offer. Be sure to let us know *all* the details to-morrow.''

Maria blushed a bright pink, snatched at her things and didn't look back as she allowed Antonio to escort her out of the office to a chorus of cheers and hoots.

"Would you like my driver to help you carry anything else down?" he asked, allowing the exaggerated accent to fade.

"Ah, no...this is fine," she said, tightly. "Let's just get on the elevator and I'll explain everything to you."

"Certainly." He let her step on ahead of him, admiring the view from behind. Yes, cashmere would suit her. She had an elegant figure. She just didn't know how to dress. Or perhaps she couldn't afford quality clothing.

As soon as the elevator doors shut, Maria faced him. "Listen, I *know* this is your job, but you can drop the phony aristocratic act now. They were just trying to embarrass me. You've done your job.'' Her chin lifted and cool mist-gray eyes darkened as if it took a great deal of courage for her to speak. And now she seemed to be struggling to hold eye contact with him. "I don't know what else you have been paid to do, but you can forget it. I don't date strange men. I have no interest in a romantic...adventure," she finished at last, looking flustered.

"You have other plans for the celebration of your birthday?" Antonio asked. "A party with your family?"

"No." She laughed as if uncomfortable that he was prolonging the conversation. "No party. I'm going home. I expect I'll enjoy my afternoon off with a good book and a hot bath."

He raised a questioning brow. "Alone?"

"Yes, *alone!*" she gasped, sounding short of breath. "What kind of woman do you take me for?"

"A lovely, intelligent, sensitive one," he said simply. He wasn't trying to flatter her; he was being perfectly honest.

After a moment, the young woman apparently realized her mouth was resting open and she brought her lips tightly together. She scowled at him. "Who *are* you, and how do I turn off the Latin-lover act?"

He refused to be offended. After all, the poor thing must be confused by all that had happened in the past twenty minutes.

"My name is Antonio Boniface, *Il Principe di Carovigno*," he explained solemnly. "I only wish to save you further harassment from your friends. And, by the way, I am an Italian citizen, not a Latin lover, as you say, and I—"

"Listen, you," she interrupted with surprising force, "I know you were hired to do a job. What do you need to prove you've done it? A signed receipt? A customer satisfaction form filled out? Just give it to me now, and I'll sign—oh my!"

They had stepped out from the lobby of the building onto Connecticut Avenue and stood on the sidewalk beside a sleek, ebony limousine. Antonio's driver had positioned himself beside the rear passenger door. He swung it open, the snappy brim of his uniform cap inclined politely toward Maria.

She swallowed and turned to Antonio, her cheeks flushed, eyes wide and glistening with childlike amazement. "Tell me this isn't part of the package."

"It's part of the package, as you put it," he said with a shrug. He always engaged a car and driver when he traveled in unfamiliar cities. At home, he preferred to drive himself in the Ferrari. There he knew the twisting coastal roads intimately and enjoyed controlling the powerful vehicle.

"Oh, jeez," she breathed. "I've never ridden in a real limo before."

He smiled, charmed by her innocence.

"Let me at least transport you home," he offered gently. "I would like to explain something to you on the way."

She hesitated. "I don't know…maybe we should just call it quits now and—"

"I wouldn't if I were you," he murmured, reaching out to take her hand again.

She nearly pulled away, then followed his gaze upward to the windows of the offices above. Rows of faces stared down at them.

"Do you want your friends to know that you've…what is the expression? Got chicken feet?"

She laughed, all the tension draining from her face. "You mean, I've chickened out…or I've gotten cold feet. No, I certainly don't want to give them that satisfaction." She shot one final grim look above them, then allowed Antonio to help her into the rear seat. Sliding across the smooth leather to give him room, she called out to the driver, "I live in Bethesda, Maryland, 755 Mullen Street. If you'll drop me off, I'll be most grateful."

He closed the door behind them, then walked around the car.

"Your driver does know where Bethesda is?" Maria asked.

"I'm sure he does. I hope it's a long ride. I have a lot to explain, Miss McPherson." Antonio smiled. He watched as her glance followed the motion of his lips.

She sighed then shook her head as if denying herself a particularly fattening dessert. "Oh my, you're awfully good. Listen, you're a very nice looking man, handsome really. And you play your role well. But I'm just not interested in your kind of…*service*."

She gave an almost imperceptible shiver of pleasure as she slipped the card Tamara had given her, unread, into her coat pocket. Her upper lip had become lightly beaded with perspiration, and her eyes were too bright. He was pretty sure she didn't even realize the signals her body was giving off.

"Maybe it would be best if we just pulled around the

block and you let me off there. I can take the bus home like I usually do."

"No," he said bluntly.

"No?" She looked alarmed now.

"On second thought," he said slowly, "I believe you deserve a real celebration. Do you have friends you'd like to invite to come along?" He could explain all about Marco, Immigration and his real identity after she'd calmed down a bit.

"Friends? No, not really. I mean, I have college friends, but they're back in Connecticut where I grew up. And the people I work with—" She shrugged as if unable to put her thoughts into words.

"They aren't like you," he supplied softly.

"No," she murmured, "they aren't like me. Take today, for instance. They get a kick out of singling out a person on their birthday and finding the most effective way to embarrass them. Tailored humiliation, I call it. I tried to take the day off, like I did last year when I'd just started working for the company, but my boss insisted she needed me." She sighed. "It's all in good fun, I suppose. But I've never liked being the center of attention."

He nodded, intrigued by her lack of ego. So unlike the women he'd known.

"So we shall celebrate quietly, just the two of us. *Si?*" His flight didn't leave until the next morning. He rarely allowed himself time away from the groves or the mill and factory. Spending an afternoon with an attractive American woman wouldn't exactly be a hardship. Besides, after handling the Marco catastrophe, he deserved a little *vacanza*.

She laughed and rolled her pretty gray eyes dramatically at him. "The two of us? Alone? Oh, I don't think so."

"Why not? A pretty woman like you deserves at least to be treated to a delicious meal in a gracious setting on her special day. Why wouldn't you allow yourself this simple pleasure?"

She gave a little growl of frustration from deep within her throat. To him it sounded delightfully sexy. "It does sound awfully tempting. I can't remember the last meal I ate out that wasn't fast food." Good, she was at least debating her decision. "This is already paid for, right? I mean, you're not going to hand me the check at the end of the meal, are you?"

He laughed. How fresh, how entertaining she was!

He had fully intended to explain about Marco, then leave her at her door. Just spiriting her off in the limo might have been enough to satisfy her work friends. But he sensed that if he took her home now, when she was questioned the next day she wouldn't lie. She would admit that she'd let her hired prince leave, then they would all feel gratified that they had sufficiently shamed her.

However, if he actually romanced her for the day, in the most innocent of ways, of course, she'd at least have a great story to tell. She'd come out the winner.

He liked that idea. She seemed such a nice person. He wanted to give her as much armor as possible against their obnoxious teasing.

Maria wrapped her arms around her body and pressed tense shoulder blades into the buttery leather cushions of the limousine. Beyond the tinted windows, the Washington cityscape passed. The famous cherry trees hadn't yet blossomed, but they were heavy with pink buds in the late morning light.

She felt awkward, out of her element. Her stomach was doing flip-flops because of her excitement. She didn't know where to put her hands, where to look...or not look. One minute her glance settled on her companion's sensuous mouth as he spoke, the next her eyes drifted to his wide, strong hands, resting on the elegant gray wool encasing his thighs.

She didn't even know his real name, and here she was ogling his *thighs!* She more than half suspected he was ready to sleep with her, might even have been paid to do so. Did she dare look at the services listed on her gift card?

Her throat and cheeks flamed at the thought. When she tried to focus on the passing Washington sights, all she saw was *his* reflection in the smoky side window of the limo. He was watching her, thinking she didn't know. The realization sent a provocative ripple of warmth down her spine where it settled in a tingling pool inside her.

"I should go home to change first," she said, glancing down at her conservative black wool dress, "if we're going anywhere fancy for lunch."

"*Prego.* Wear something that makes you feel feminine and happy," he suggested in a rich baritone.

She tried to ignore the way his words resonated pleasantly along her nerves. Sort of tickling. Sort of nice. What *would* she wear?

Nearly everything she owned was black or shades of neutral. Work clothes, chosen not to attract attention, to give her a professional appearance and avoid feminine vulnerability. Or else jeans and sweatshirts—those were for weekends. There had never been a reason to buy anything else, even if she could have afforded more. Maybe Sarah, her neighbor, would lend her one of her scores of dresses. Something at least with a little color in it.

"You'd look good in—" he seemed to be considering options "—perhaps an Ungaro, or a Dolce frock. Or one of the newer styles I've seen from Positano."

"Positano?" She laughed, remembering a recent article in *Vogue* that she'd drooled over. "As in Italy and ultrahigh couture? Listen, you don't have to keep up the act for my benefit."

"I don't?" He lifted heavy, dark brows. There was a hint of amusement on his full lips.

"Of course not. I know you're from around here, hired to escort me." She brought out the card and flicked it at him. "The polite way of saying *date* me for money." She gave him an understanding smile to let him know there were no bad feelings. "A prince? That's honestly how your agency bills you?"

"That's who I am," he said mildly. He took the card from her and slipped it into his suit jacket pocket.

She gave a little snort. "*Prince,* indeed. Titles went out of style with fairy tales. Don't they know that?"

"I wasn't aware."

She told herself she should hate the smug way he was observing her. But he was just so delicious to look at, it was hard to find fault with him.

Thirty minutes later they arrived at her apartment house. Maria slid closer to the door. The driver moved quickly, opening it for her. She felt Antonio come across the seat after her.

"*You* stay *here,*" she instructed him firmly, as if he were a mischievous puppy being told to *heel.*

"Escorting the lady to her door is the gentlemanly thing to do," he objected, looking disappointed.

"Yeah, well, gentlemanly or not, you're waiting in the car."

She wasn't about to let a call boy, or however they referred to themselves, into her apartment. Things were already complicated enough with him sitting on her street in a limousine.

It was a good thing most of her neighbors were at work. Someone was bound to be home, though. She wondered if she told Mrs. Kranski in 7B (who was undoubtedly staring out her window even now) that she was attending a funeral, would the woman believe her?

Maria punched in the security code and let herself into the building. She hit 8 in the elevator, tapped her foot impatiently as she rose to her floor. Another second and she was through her front door, breathing raggedly.

Was she insane? Agreeing to go with this stranger to her own private birthday celebration. But maybe she could pull this off. Just go out for lunch with the guy, give him as generous a tip as her weekly budget would allow, then be back before six when most of her neighbors arrived home.

Ten minutes later, she'd donned a nubby purple sweater and black wool skirt. Conservative black, low-heeled pumps. Off-black panty hose. Her only real gold jewelry (the tiny heart-shaped studs she'd gotten free when she'd had her ears pierced) and a fresh application of makeup completed the job.

She was ready for anything!

Anything, she realized when she returned to the car, except for this amazingly gorgeous man, whoever he really was. When he saw her coming down the steps to the sidewalk, he signaled his driver who swung the passenger door wide with a flourish. Her date stood up out of the car to let her pass, then held out a hand to guide her down and into the limousine.

"They certainly do train you guys well, I'll say that much," she murmured as she slipped back across the lake of gray leather.

"Mi scusi?" He sat beside her.

"Well," she began nervously, "it's just that practically no one has good, old-fashioned manners these days. My mother used to complain about that all the time." She knew she was babbling, but she had to keep talking to control the runaway pace of her heart. "By the way, what should I call you, Prince?" She grinned, feeling silly just saying it.

He was looking at her *that way* again. As if she amused him. It wasn't that she minded being entertaining. It was just that she so infrequently got that sort of reaction from men. From anyone.

"Antonio," he said at last. "That's my real name."

"Oh." Maybe it was.

"Your mother lives near you?" he asked.

"No," she said regretfully, as the car pulled smoothly

away from the curb. "My mother died two years ago. Cancer."

"I'm sorry," he said softly.

She was aware that he was observing her very closely. She blinked twice, taking care of the threat of tears. "It was hard. For both of us. We were close."

"But for comfort you have the rest of your family—"

She was already shaking her head. "No one really close. But it's okay. My father was never in the picture, and I was an only child. I have an aunt in Connecticut. We send Christmas cards," she added with an effort to sound brighter.

"So you're alone," he said, "truly alone."

She glanced across the car at him, and she could have sworn there was honest sympathy reflected in his eyes. Strange, she thought, someone in his line of work caring at all. After a while, she would have thought men like him would have become immune to their clients' personal traumas. Sort of like bartenders.

"I have my work. It can be satisfying." She slanted a quick look at him without turning her head. She could feel him still watching her. She wondered why he'd suddenly gone quiet, and what he was thinking.

A moment later Antonio sat forward on the seat and spoke quietly to the driver. She couldn't make out his words.

They drove toward the center of the city, gliding over Wisconsin Avenue, through fashionable Chevy Chase. The car finally pulled up in front of a store she'd passed by many times but never would have dared step inside.

"Versace isn't a restaurant," she said helpfully.

"I know. But I've changed my plans. Where we're going, you'll feel more comfortable wearing something different."

She looked down at her outfit. "This isn't dressy enough?"

He tipped his head to one side and observed her objectively. "It doesn't do you justice," he stated. "Come. You decide after you've tried on a few pieces."

Maria let out an involuntary little snort. "Now I know *this* isn't part of the package deal. My office pals would never spring for anything this extravagant. Do you realize what stuff in a place like this costs?"

"It will be taken care of," he said simply.

She stared at him then smiled, feeling a little daring. "All right. If you're game, so am I. But no one in Versace is coming within ten feet of my charge card!"

He laughed and shook his head at her. "Agreed, *cara*."

An hour later they left Versace Couture with a slim gold box, in which Maria's old clothes, shoes and hose had been packed beneath shimmering layers of tissue. She wore an elegant powder-blue, cashmere suit with a gold brooch, and sleek Italian leather slings with tiny heels. All purchased for her through a mysterious arrangement between Antonio and the saleswoman that involved only a signature and not even a glimpse of a check or plastic. The sales staff all but genuflected as he left the boutique.

Maria had become a believer. Almost.

If he wasn't actual royalty (which she still found hard to accept), he at least had one soaring credit allowance and the respect of high-end merchants—neither of which was likely to come as a perk for working as a professional escort.

This took serious mental adjustments.

Next stop was I Matti, an upscale Tuscan-style trattoria, on Eighteenth Street. Antonio ordered for her, and she was delighted with his choices. They dined on lamb shanks and pasta with a heady tomato sauce redolent with olive oil, accompanied by a delicious Barolo wine.

She couldn't help questioning him further. "You're really Italian then," she said as they returned to the limousine.

"Yes."

"And rich?"

"Very." He seemed more amused than offended by her questions.

She nodded, thinking about times in the distant past when she'd been called gullible.

She had fallen for Donny Apericcio's game, playing Doctor and Patient, when she was seven. She'd had to undress to be "treated" for her pretend ailment. And she had believed Becky Feinstein in high school when the popular girl had congratulated Maria on making the yearbook committee. It had been a cruel joke.

But those episodes were kids' stuff, embarrassments she'd gotten over long ago. Allowing herself to be charmed, possibly even seduced by a stranger, was of the adult world. A game she wasn't about to play with any man, rich or not.

"So-o-o-o," she said pushing Antonio's wide hand off of her knee where it had wandered as soon as they'd seated themselves in the limo. "You're an honest-to-goodness prince, and you have a perfectly reasonable explanation for why you're in this country, standing in for a paid date."

"*Si,* my former valet, he was posing as me and causing my family terrible embarrassment."

"Valet," she repeated thoughtfully. "And what do you do in Italy? Own a vineyard or something?"

"Olive groves, a mill where the olives are crushed for their oil, and a bottling factory," he corrected her, smiling proudly. "Passed down many generations through my family."

She absorbed these new details. "Listen, I hope you'll understand my confusion. I didn't know you, but I do know my co-workers. They once hired a stripper dressed up like a pizza delivery person to surprise a man who was retiring. Then there was the singing kangaroo."

"Kangaroo?"

"You don't want to know," she assured him with a roll of her eyes. "The thing is, I'm going along with this for one reason only. To save myself grief in the office."

He looked a little disappointed. "I thought you were coming with me because you'd never ridden in a limousine."

"That too," she admitted quickly, uncomfortable that he'd remembered an unguarded moment of girlish enthusiasm. "But I really don't need all this wining and dining stuff to be happy on my birthday. A good book and a hot bubble bath are just fine. And I don't mind being alone," she added quickly when he opened his mouth as if to comment. "I *enjoy* my privacy."

Which was true. To a certain degree.

She'd always needed time to herself. Time to read, to write in her journal, to garden or listen without interruptions to a CD of her favorite opera. A cup of sweet tea and a melt-your-knees tenor singing to her while she soaked in steaming water was her idea of heaven.

But there were times, more and more often these days, when she'd have liked someone to eat dinner with, someone to talk to about her day or snuggle up with in bed at night before falling asleep. These were other kinds of quiet times.

Sex? The word popped into her head. Sex would be nice, she imagined.

Everyone said it was an indispensable part of life, although she believed most people made too much of it. Someday she'd be able to judge for herself. That time would come when she found the man she would marry.

Until then, she had promised herself she wouldn't surrender totally to any man. Her mother had made that mistake, and had been left alone with a baby. Maria admitted to herself that she was curious, maybe even a little anxious as the months and years wore on and she felt child-bearing years slipping away from her. But she wouldn't be foolish.

Antonio's hand returned to her knee. This time she eyed it thoughtfully, but didn't brush it off. "Where to next?" she asked.

"Next, we go to Espazio Italia. On my last trip to this country I saw there the loveliest terra-cotta pieces outside of my own country. I would like to buy presents for family back home and, if you like, something for you as well."

She shrugged, having already decided it was easier to go along with him than fight a mulish man. "Sounds harmless enough. Why not?"

So why did she feel as if she'd just stepped off a cliff into thin air? Why did her instincts shriek at her that, with that simple gesture of lifted shoulders, she had just set forces in motion over which she had no control?

TWO

Maria was delighted by the profusion of amazing hand-made pottery from Sicily, Taormina and Grottaglie. The brilliant colors evoked Mediterranean sunshine and made her feel cheerful just by looking at them.

Antonio bought a pretty glazed bowl and a small figurine of an ebony horse, and had them wrapped—for safe travel, he told the clerk. It seemed odd that he was purchasing items that had originated in his own country, but maybe he was too busy with his olive groves to go shopping very often at home.

He offered to buy Maria a pretty vase she had admired, but she politely refused after flipping over the price tag. "I'll save up for it and come back someday." But she knew she never would. Everything in the shop was gorgeous but way out of her budget's league.

At last they drove back across the city as the sun set, and Maria felt as if she were melting into the limousine's seats. She hadn't felt so relaxed, so pleased with a day in as long as she could remember. If humiliating her had been her friends' goal, their plan had failed miserably. This day and Antonio had been wonderful gifts.

The car pulled up in front of her apartment building. Maria sat up straight and was about to turn toward the passenger door beside her when Antonio's hand closed around the back of her neck and easily guided her back toward him.

"Sei bellissima," he murmured, then kissed her expertly, softly on the lips.

It happened so fast, she didn't have time to draw a breath or protest. When he pulled back a few inches to observe her reaction, she was speechless.

"You still don't believe me," he said. "I can see it in your face."

She shrugged, but the words came out in a froggy little whisper. "I believe you're Antonio Boniface from Italy. It's the prince part that's still a little hard to swallow."

"A pity you're such a cautious woman." He tapped one finger on her chin, her cheek, then the sensitive lobe of one ear.

"What's wrong with being cautious?" she asked, mesmerized by his voice as much as by his touch.

"You will miss out on a lot of life's pleasures."

She laughed nervously, her heart thudding in her chest. "I don't suppose we're talking about chocolate cake or a good movie?"

"No." He gave her an amused smile.

"Listen," she said over a sudden dry spot in her throat, "I think I know what you're getting at. I'm just not in the habit of sleeping around."

"I know that." His finger continued its path, tracing her lips, trailing down her throat.

She gulped. "You do?"

He nodded slowly. "You're easy to read, Maria McPherson. You were an obedient child, and now you're a careful woman. You don't entice men, intentionally that is. In fact—''

He studied her face thoughtfully, then ran an experimental hand around behind her neck and brought his fingers up through the strands of her hair at her nape. The sensation was electric. She shivered deliciously.

''In fact, I wonder if you've not been too careful.''

''In, ah…in what way?'' she asked breathlessly.

''In the way of totally avoiding satisfaction. By running from the joy of sharing yourself with a man.''

He was asking if she was a virgin. ''This is getting way…way too personal,'' she stammered.

He smiled apologetically but didn't remove his hand. It felt pleasantly rough, not what she'd expected of gentry, if he was that. His fingers tangled playfully in her blond waves.

''Only an observation. I'm fascinated by your decision. If you elect to wait for your life mate, that is an honorable choice—one which any man should respect. I only wonder that a lovely woman like you shouldn't be more eager to experiment a little.''

''I didn't say I wasn't *curious*,'' Maria blurted out, then realized she had made a tactical error in this matching of wits.

She suddenly wondered where the driver had gone. He was no longer in the front seat, but he didn't seem to be waiting outside her door either.

''I mean, of course, *anyone* is curious about something they've never tried, something everyone talks about and requires at least one scene in every movie you see. That would be natural.''

''Of course,'' he said. ''Natural.'' There, again, was that enigma of a smile. He didn't insist upon an explanation, but she felt compelled to give one.

''Listen, my not wanting to have sex with you, a stranger, if that's what you're hinting at, has nothing to do with how attractive you are. Believe me, if I were to choose a man on looks alone, he'd be someone like you. On top of that, you have great manners and that super accent, and you're fun to be around.''

''But you wouldn't sleep with me?'' He was teasing her, yet he was also serious. She could see mixed motives in the dark glitter of his oh-so-blue eyes.

''No!'' she gasped. ''I don't even know you, Antonio. For goodness' sakes, you could be married!''

''I've been honest, I told you my name and where I'm from. Now I add that I'm not married. *Dio!* I can see you still don't fully believe me.'' He sounded honestly frustrated. ''How can we get to know each other? You tell me.''

She let out a long, weary breath. After all, she didn't want to hurt the man's feelings. ''Listen, come upstairs for a cup of coffee. I think I have a pound cake in the freezer. But this is just a way for us to talk, okay? I'm not luring you up to my apartment to have my way with you.''

''Certainly not,'' he said, agreeably.

''Or to let you have your way with me,'' she added, just to make things perfectly clear.

But she feared all her warnings were doing no good. The dangerous twinkle in his eyes worried her. On the other hand, she'd already decided he wasn't a threat. And even if he were, the walls of her apartment were onion-skin thin. One scream would bring three sets of neighbors running to her aid with the police soon to follow. Neighbors looked after each other in Bethesda.

She opened the door that led straight into her living room and turned, by habit, to lock the door behind them. Almost at once, she felt Antonio move up close behind her. She could feel his breath on the back of her neck, warm, inviting her to turn to face him.

If she didn't take evasive action, he'd kiss her again. She

stepped to one side, ducked, maneuvered around him and aimed for her kitchen.

He didn't follow her, as she feared he might. Instead, he strolled around her little apartment checking out her knick-knacks—her collection of seashells, her dainty demitasse cups and saucers displayed on their own cherry wood wall rack—while she made coffee and nuked a Sara Lee.

Finally, they sat on her couch and sipped and nibbled in electric silence. She thought she could hear her own heart-beat drumming in her ears. Her palms were moist and hot.

It was she, despite all common sense, who returned to their earlier conversation. "It's just that I believe sex to be only one factor in a complex relationship that develops, over time, into marriage. My mother had me when she was very young. She never went to college because of me. Her whole life was different than it might have been because I came along, because my father disappeared when she told him she was pregnant."

"And she supported both herself and you on her own?" he asked.

"Yes. It must have been terribly hard for her. I just don't want it to be like that for me, raising a child alone. I want a husband first, then children. Everything in its proper or-der, you see?"

He took a bite of cake then nodded thoughtfully. "I un-derstand."

"But, you're right, a person can't help being curious. I mean, at work every day, people tell jokes then look at me to see if I get them. They know, I guess, that I'm sort of…inexperienced, and it amuses them."

"You're charming," Antonio murmured, a smile lifting the corners of his lips.

"And *you* have a one-track mind." She rolled her eyes then laughed at his hurt expression.

He put his plate on the coffee table and leaned toward her, his wide hands braced on his knees. "I'm not as obsessed with sex as you imagine. I just haven't had much time or desire to be with a pretty woman, not for several years now."

She pinched off a morsel of cake to plop into her mouth. He certainly was an unusual man. Not at all easy to figure out. No woman in years?

"Are you telling me you're no longer just trying to make up for what your former employee did? The time you're spending with me now is personal?"

"It always was." Before she could figure out what that was supposed to mean, he looked away from her so that she couldn't read his expression. "Tell me, what will happen when you return to work?"

Maria grimaced. "Oh, they'll bombard me with questions. They'll demand to know everywhere we went and everything we did."

"And you will say?"

"I'll tell them about the restaurant and the lovely meal, about the clothes and seeing the beautiful ceramics."

"But they will pester you for more, for they'll want to hear what occurred *later*."

"Yes, I suppose they will." The thought made her uncomfortable even now. "But I'll tell them nothing happened."

He nodded. "*Si*. And they will laugh. Again."

"I suppose."

She stared down at her half-eaten cake, then impatiently shoved the plate off her lap and onto the table in front of her. A daring thought struck her.

"I could make up something. What do you think? Maybe if I told them racy tidbits about you and me in bed, then they'd leave me alone. They'd see that their plan to embarrass me had backfired."

"How good are you at lying?" he asked.

She pursed her lips and considered. "Not very."

"So you have a problem." He stood up and walked to the only window in the room.

It overlooked the side of another red-brick building. He stared through the glass pane as if at a breathtaking vista. She knew his mind must be elsewhere, and she couldn't blame him. They were of two vastly different worlds. He was probably bored to tears with her.

"Call your office and leave a message that you won't be in tomorrow," he said abruptly.

She laughed. "Why would I do that?"

He turned to face her, his eyes bright with fun, devious with mystery. "Because you're having an affair."

"What?"

"Because you can't bear to leave the arms of the man who has made passionate love to you all afternoon."

She choked over her response. "You're insane!"

Rushing to her he pulled her off the couch. "Do you want to return to them as the meek, cowed Maria? The helpless target of their humor?"

"Well, no, but I'll have to go back sooner or later. It is my job, after all. They'll only need to look at me to know that nothing happened."

"Exactly," he agreed.

Maria thoughtfully chewed the tip of one fingernail, but it didn't help. "If there were some way to learn what it is like...you know, to learn without actually *doing it*."

"Well, there are certain films. But these aren't the sort of things a woman of your caliber should be exposed to."

"I'm not even sure I'd want to watch other people...you know." She felt a wave of heat rise up her throat. "Well, I'm not going to give myself to any man unless we're married," she repeated, "so that's that."

"Not entirely."

She squinted up at Antonio warily. Donny Apericcio came fleetingly to mind. "If this is a trick to get me into bed—"

"No trick, just a suggestion."

She just glared at him.

He seemed oblivious to her lack of enthusiasm. "I assume you haven't reached the age of twenty-two without being kissed?"

"I'm twenty-five, thank you. And yes, of course I've been kissed…and I've kissed back plenty of times," she defended herself.

"Good. Have you touched a man and let him touch you?"

"You mean, petted?" She knew she was blushing furiously now. "Sure. A little. It was okay."

"If it was just *okay,* you haven't really been touched," he said, his voice lowering to a husky mellowness.

If he'd been standing closer to her, she would have evaporated. Even at the distance of half a room away, a pleasant warmth rippled through her. She winced, willing her body to behave itself. "I'm not sure what you're suggesting, exactly."

"I'm offering to demonstrate to you how it is—between a man and a woman—without risking your virginity. I could teach you, *cara.*"

She swallowed, her eyes widening despite her attempt to remain composed. She suddenly felt as limp as an overcooked noodle. "I don't think this is a good idea. Even talking like this isn't a good idea."

She started to cross the room toward the door, having decided to ask him to leave. But Antonio moved quickly in front of her. She came to an abrupt and graceless halt within inches of his broad chest. He was so near she could feel the heat of his body through their clothing.

"I wouldn't hurt you. I would stop immediately if anything I said or did offended you," he promised.

She frowned. Why was this sounding like a win-win situation? Why was she even *considering* such an outlandish proposal?

Because, she answered her own questions, she liked him. And she really was curious. Had been for as long as she could remember.

She wanted to know what her husband would look like and do on the first night of their honeymoon. Wanted to be ready to respond to him appropriately, to please him.

At first, she had told herself that was one of the exciting things about getting married—not knowing, looking forward to the unpredictable, the new. But as time passed and she met no one who even remotely interested her in a serious, marriagelike way, she began to wonder if she was holding out for the wrong reasons. Was it only because she was afraid?

She looked at Antonio. He was watching her closely.

"Maybe if we'd known each other for a long time. Then this experiment of yours might be something to at least consider. There would be an automatic sense of trust."

"Call your office," he whispered. "Tell them you won't be in tomorrow."

She couldn't take her eyes off of him. Couldn't seem to draw another breath while she was caught up in the intensity of his gaze.

This is crazy, she told herself. This is impulsive and dangerous and…and, dammit, exciting!

Yes, she had to admit, she was intrigued by his proposition. And although she knew it sounded a bit crazy, she was reassured by the man who proposed it. There was something very agreeable about Antonio. He was serious, quiet, obviously well-educated and intelligent. And he was generous with his time and money. In short, he felt safe.

But aside from all that, she'd never met a man as physically appealing or as aware of his power over women. She'd seen the looks he'd gotten from women in the restaurant and shops they'd visited. She wasn't the only one attracted to him. He knew it. But he hadn't shown it.

She'd bet if anyone knew about making love, Antonio would.

"I'll call in!" The words burst impulsively from her lips, but she reined in her runaway hormones almost immediately. "We can spend tomorrow together. Doing fun stuff like today. But the rest of it…that demonstrating part…" She shook her head.

He nodded, his expression composed, revealing nothing of his thoughts. "As you wish. Tomorrow we will visit a few museums, have lunch, talk about life." He gave her an encouraging smile.

"It sounds very nice," she admitted releasing a breath she'd held so long she'd begun to feel lightheaded. "No more sex talk, right?"

"Not a word," he agreed, solemnly.

She studied his expression a moment longer. She believed him.

So why did her body tingle as if his palms—as strong and weathered as the bark of his olive trees—were moving over the surface of her flesh? Why did she sense that they'd already entered a silent pact, whose terms she couldn't yet read?

Antonio stood before the painting he had most looked forward to seeing that day. It was in a collection temporarily loaned to the National Gallery of Art—Portraits of Italian Renaissance Women. When he'd first seen Maria, this was the painting that had made him wonder if he'd met her before.

Now Maria stood beside him gazing up at the proud woman's delicate features, and he was entranced by her reactions. She frowned, concentrating. Her arms were folded across her body, hugging herself.

"What are you thinking?" he asked.

She tilted her head slowly, side to side. "I don't know. This one seems so real, so modern in a way. But I can't put my finger on why. Is it because da Vinci's style bridges the centuries?''

The picture was labeled, *Portrait of Genevra de Benci,* signed by the master. Antonio had viewed it many times in his own country. His mother had first pointed it out to him, as she and the model shared the same first name. There the resemblance ended.

The portrait was exquisite, not only because of the famous painter's talent but because of the simple, natural beauty of the woman who sat for him.

"Perhaps," he said, "it's a combination of his artistry and the woman's beauty. Tell me what you see when you look at it.''

Maria gave him a puzzled look but didn't object to the exercise. He moved closer to her, as if to better hear her lowered voice in the museum's hushed exhibit room. He liked the way she smelled of soap and baby powder. Simple yet erotic fragrances. He focused on the smooth curve of her throat, so similar to that of the portrait before them.

"Well," she murmured, "her hair is shining and pale, elaborate braids woven with those strands of baby pearls and satin ribbons. And she wears a choker of gold chains clasped with a cameo at her throat. The blond hair—" She squinted thoughtfully at the graceful coils lifted above the subject's head. "She must have been considered a rare beauty back then.''

"Yes, Italians are drawn to light complexions, to pale-haired women and children. Back then, before chemical hair dyes, they were probably rare for my part of the world.''

"Her dress is beautiful. A kind of rich brocade, with lace panels.''

"Another sign of her wealth," he agreed.

"There's something else.'' Her frown deepened, intensified.

"Do you not yet see it?" he asked, moving still closer until his lips nearly brushed the rim of her ear.

Maria's eyes slowly cleared then widened. "You're not thinking that there's a resemblance between her and me!"

"Most definitely, there is," he said, pleased that she'd finally seen the similarity, although she denied it. He gently lifted heavy strands of hair from her neck and held them in a soft coil above her head. "Look at me, *cara.*"

She turned self-consciously. "Antonio," she whispered, "people are watching us."

"It's of no matter." He smiled. "I'm just looking at another Renaissance woman. The room is full of them."

She laughed, embarrassed, and brushed his hands away. "I've been having so much fun today, I forgot that flattering a woman comes easily to you."

She was wrong.

How long had it been since he'd bothered to even look at a woman with any interest? Not since Anna died had he allowed himself such pleasure. But Maria was more than physically attractive. He had felt very close to her since first seeing her. Only later had he realized why.

The painting.

The de Benci family was linked with his own through marriage. Genevra had wed a distant relation of his southern Italian ancestors. She, so the story went, came from the north, from a family of less wealth than the de Bencis. But her husband loved her deeply and had given her pearls, jewels, and expensive silks for her gowns. She had returned his affection by wearing his gifts every day—around her throat, in her blond tresses, on her fingers and curling round her tiny wrists.

Antonio imagined strings of tiny pearls woven through Maria's pale hair. He closed his eyes and was nearly overcome by a wave of desire. He snapped his eyes open immediately.

Why now? Why two long years after losing Anna was

he allowing a stranger from another country to affect him this way? This was not a woman to have an affair with. This was not a woman to soothe his tormented soul. She was looking for a husband, and he would never marry again.

A cold hand closed around his heart. He set his jaw and moved away from Maria. After a moment, she followed him to stand before a bust of a patrician lady. She was silent, as if thinking thoughts as deep as his.

Neither spoke again while in the museum.

They drove next to the private Corcoran Gallery. Antonio silently led her through rooms displaying rare Greek and Roman antiquities.

She spotted several examples of brilliantly glazed Italian majolica of a more recent era. "They're gorgeous!" She traced a bunch of rich purple ceramic grapes with one fingertip. "You only have to look at these to be happy," she bubbled.

He stared at her, amazed. It took so little to make the woman happy? But yes, he could see it in her soft gray eyes—pure gladness, simple joy over an exquisite bowl. He wished life could be that easy for him.

For several minutes he felt as if he couldn't breathe. The atrium into which he'd stepped went dark around him. He stood gazing out at the gardens without seeing them. The sadness was suddenly overwhelming.

After some time, he became aware of Maria standing beside him. He hadn't heard her approach.

"Are you all right? Did I say something to upset you?" she asked cautiously.

He couldn't speak for a moment. "It's nothing. I'm sorry if I've spoiled your day."

She laughed. "You haven't spoiled my day at all. Listen, I haven't had this much fun in as long as I can remember. Ever maybe. You're great company, Antonio. I just wish I took the time to museum crawl more often. I should. It's not as if it costs much."

"I should too," he said, testing his voice, relieved to find it didn't break. "I should live again."

"What?" She frowned at him.

"Never mind, *cara.* Let's have lunch. I know just the place. You will love it."

He took her to Coeur de Lion, a popular city restaurant he hoped to make one of his first American clients. His plan was to introduce Boniface Olive Oils to the U.S. market through fine restaurants.

The Coeur de Lion's vaulted ceiling with its sunshine-filled skylight brightened his mood. Besides, he was determined to not rain on Maria's day, a continuation of her birthday celebration.

They sat on tufted chairs at a table apart from the others, covered with a heavy white damask cloth. He told her stories of Apulia, his ancient homeland in Italy, and she listened intently.

Tomorrow, he thought, I will be gone. He'd rescheduled his flight again, but would delay his return no longer than that. Now that Marco had been dealt with, he needed to return to the groves. Although it was still barely spring in Washington, already there was important work to be done in Carovigno.

By the time they left the restaurant and had driven back to her apartment, it was nearly three in the afternoon.

"I shouldn't have had so much wine." Maria giggled as she fumbled her key into the lock. "I'm going to be sleepy before dinnertime, though I don't think I could eat another bite all day. Oh, that was delicious!"

He smiled, took the key from her and let her into her apartment. She spun around twice before flopping like a little child on her couch and laughing to herself—a final comment on the fun of the day before letting her eyes drift drowsily closed.

"You're leaving now, aren't you?" she asked without opening them.

"Yes," he said, with honest regret, "I should."

She nodded. "Probably best."

"Probably?" He frowned. Was she sending him a different message now? "I thought you didn't want my company other than as a touring companion."

"Didn't…don't…not sure anymore." She sighed and opened her eyes with obvious effort to nibble at a corner of one fingernail, her brow delicately furrowed. "Must be the wine talking. It's just that I was thinking last night, after you left— No, I can't say that."

"Say what?" he asked, smiling indulgently at her confusion.

Her cheeks flushed a pretty pink. "I wouldn't want you to get the wrong idea. But the concept…the *theory* of being coached, so to speak… Well, it appeals to me."

He laughed softly but felt a nearly forgotten masculine tug down low in his body. "Does it now? But you said you'd have to know me better to trust me."

"Yes, I did." She seemed to be having trouble remembering her earlier statements through the wine. "I definitely said that. And it's true, you need to trust a person to be intimate with them. Don't you?"

"It's wise," he agreed, walking closer to her and dropping her keys on the coffee table in front of her. "Especially for a woman."

"Yes, and espe—" She had trouble getting that word untangled from her tongue. "—es-pe-cially when that other person has had a lot more experience than you. Experience in activities that might cause him to be exposed to dangerous viral things and such."

"You needn't worry about that with me," he assured her.

"Why not?"

He loved the way she scowled at him, her lips pouting,

her brow wrinkling, a shadow of the little girl...inside the body of a woman. He ached to kiss her, but wouldn't take advantage of her. The wine's effect hadn't yet begun to wane.

"Because I have been very careful," he stated. Because, he could have added, there has been no one to share my bed in two full years. And for the five years before Anna died, he'd been only with her. "Let's just say, I'm safe. But if the situation arose, I'd still use protection to ease your concern."

"Of course you would." She pulled a tasseled pillow toward her and hugged it so hard he wondered if the seams might pop. She squinted up at him speculatively. "If the situation arose," she echoed him. "But your teaching...well, it wouldn't include that *arising* stuff, right?"

He laughed delightedly and shook his finger at her. "*Signorina,* something definitely would rise, but we wouldn't *go all the way,* as you say in this country."

Her brow smoothed. "That's right. We wouldn't. So there would be no need at all to worry. Would there?"

"None."

"All right," she said, looking suddenly wide-awake and sober as she pushed the pillow away. "Let's go for it." She smiled up at him.

He was shocked. *"Aspetta un momento!* I thought you didn't want to...that you were saving yourself for—"

"I am. Of course I am. I just want you to show me what I need to know. Everything except the end part." She looked up at him solemnly.

He roared with laughter. "You don't know what you're saying. You've had too much wine, Maria. Tomorrow you'll regret asking this of me."

"I will?" She pouted again, and he nearly dragged her into his arms then and there.

"Yes," he said softly. He took her hand, sat on the couch beside her and drew her close. "We will sit quietly together, let the wine wear off. If you feel the same way after another hour, we'll do whatever you decide.''

She looked up at him with wide, trusting eyes. ''All right.''

Maria wasn't aware of the moment when her eyelids floated shut, or when she first awoke. The subtle lingering scent of a man's aftershave came to her, then the sense that the surface beneath her was shifting.

Her eyes flashed open. ''Antonio!''

''Yes?'' a deep voice answered from above her.

She rolled over to discover that she'd been lying with her cheek pressed into his lap. She sat up abruptly, causing him to lift his arm, which had been draped protectively over her.

''You're still here. What time is it?''

''Nearly five-thirty,'' he said.

''I slept for over two hours?''

''*Si*. I took a little nap too. Sitting up.''

She had slept with a stranger in the room…with a stranger *under* her. Unexpectedly, the intimacy warmed rather than frightened her.

''Thank you for staying,'' she whispered.

''I wouldn't have left without saying goodbye,'' he assured her.

''Then you *are* leaving?''

''That's what you want, isn't it?'' He tenderly touched the tip of her nose, just once, with his long finger. ''Do you remember what you asked of me before you fell asleep?''

She did. *Vividly*.

And, strangely enough, the only thing that had changed was her confidence that she could handle the lessons she'd requested of him.

''I remember,'' she said, watching his expression. ''I'd still like you to show me. I'm just not sure how.''

He observed her for a long time before answering. ''It's

up to the man to know how. It's up to you, the woman, only to say yes or no.''

A rush of heat swept through her body. When she tried to speak, the words dried up before crossing her lips. At last she managed the only ones that seemed important. ''Then I say…*yes.*''

He nodded solemnly, no longer questioning her. Gently, he lifted her out of his lap. He stood up. ''Then we must do this right.''

She watched from the couch as he put on his coat and moved toward the door. A wave of panic and disappointment swept over her. ''Where are you going?''

''Shopping,'' he said, scooping up her keys. ''I'll be back in an hour. While I am gone—'' He returned to drop a kiss on her upturned forehead. ''—you will take one of your long, hot baths. But you will not read a book.''

''I won't?''

''No. You will think of me.'' Looking deeply into her eyes, he kissed her again quickly on the lips. ''Imagine my body and your body. Think about kisses that last so long you become faint with lack of oxygen.''

Then he was gone.

Maria stared at the door—her throat parched, hands trembling, heart racing.

Good grief. What had she done?

Three

The bath was still steaming around her when Maria heard her apartment door open and close, then the latch turn. Sitting up in the tub she listened.

Keys clinked on the coffee table. Bags rustled. Footsteps—a man's by the weight of them—crossed her living room to her kitchen. She swallowed nervously, once, then again when the lump in her throat didn't go away.

There was a gentle knock on the bathroom door. Hastily, Maria slid with a slosh beneath the thick blanket of bubbles. "Yes?"

"I have something for you to put on when you're ready." A hand slipped through the crack between the door and the wall, slid a parcel onto the towel shelf. Masculine fingers retracted then appeared again—this time with a champagne flute, filled with liquid gold. "Take your time."

Positively dizzy with apprehension, she managed to haul herself out of the tub. However, as she dried off then, wrapped in her towel, opened the package and sipped her champagne, she began to feel a little braver. Her persistent curiosity was returning.

She had done as Antonio had asked. She had closed her eyes while soaking in the warm water and imagined a man's body. She also had thought about the places on her own body where no one's hand but her own had touched.

She tingled with anticipation.

From the rose-colored box she lifted a layer of pink tissue. Beneath it lay lingerie so delicate, so ethereal it barely whispered through her fingers. She looked at the label, knowing what it would say before she read it—silk. Pure shimmering, eggshell silk, with elegant borders of ecru lace.

She powdered herself and slipped on the delectable creation. It covered her in one long flow of fabric from breasts to ankles, but the contours of her body and her raised nipples showed through. She'd never owned anything so luxurious. So sensual.

When her hair was dry she applied lip gloss and a featherlight coat of mascara. Finally, she took a deep breath and, bringing with her the last of her champagne, stepped out of the bathroom.

She didn't know what she expected. Antonio in skin-tight briefs? Antonio in the nude? But she found him sitting on her couch, in nearly the same position as before. When he heard her, he stood and gazed approvingly at her, then raised his glass.

"*Sei bellissima.* You are a beautiful woman, Maria."

She blinked at him, not believing but pleased none the less. "You've changed your clothes too," she observed. He was wearing slate-hued slacks with a soft caramel-colored sweater that she was sure must be cashmere. The shirt collar was dazzling white, crisp and open, no confining tie.

"I returned to my room to shower and change. I wanted to be fresh for you."

"That was a nice gesture," she said, "as are the gown and the champagne. Antonio, I want to help you pay for all of this, it's really generous of you but it would be wrong of me to expect you—"

He waved off her offer. "The cost is of no concern. Come."

Standing, he walked toward the kitchenette bar that separated her living room from the food prep area and motioned to her to join him. He'd laid out a bowl of huge strawberries and a dish of whipped cream. Dipping the tip of a strawberry into the frothy mixture, he fed her one.

"Part of the lessons," he explained.

The fruit was ripe, juicy and delicious, but when he offered her a second she held up a hand.

"Are you having second thoughts?" he asked.

"No," she answered quickly. But maybe she was. For her feelings were as hard to grasp as if they were a beam of light splintered by a prism into separate bands of color. She could see each individual hue, but what they might form when refocused into the bright, white light of day, she couldn't say.

He touched her shoulder encouragingly. "We can just talk, if you prefer."

She looked down at his hand. He wore no wedding band, nor was there an indentation to show that he had recently removed one. He had said he wasn't married, but she had trouble imagining him without a beautiful woman on his arm. He was just too damn good looking to be on his own for long.

She braced one hip on a high stool at the breakfast bar. "Tell me, Antonio," she began nervously, "when you make love to a woman, what do you do first?"

"We talk and enjoy something light and delicious to eat, as we are now. Perhaps there is wine, perhaps a little music." Sweeping her suddenly off the stool and into his arms he demonstrated by spinning her around in a dizzying, musicless waltz. "We dance."

She laughed, delighted. "And then?"

"That depends. I might touch her softly. Here." He smoothed the back of his curled fingers across her collarbone, her shoulder, then down the sensitive swell along the outside of her breast. Her flesh warmed beneath his hand. She hissed an involuntary breath between her teeth. "Then I pay close attention to her reaction."

Maria smiled weakly at him. "That kind of reaction?"

He nodded, looking pleased. *"Si."*

"Then what?"

"If she responded with pleasure at my touch—" He looked thoughtful, as if trying to remember steps to a once-familiar dance.

She stared into his midnight-blue eyes, fascinated, wondering what he was thinking and why he hesitated. Even though she had assured him that she wanted him to show her these things.

"If she seemed amenable," he began again, "I would kiss her."

"On the mouth?" she asked when he didn't immediately suit action to words.

"For the moment, yes." His gaze glittered with interesting highlights and even more interesting secrets.

It seemed to her that she was now leading this dance of theirs. And for some reason that seemed all wrong, all backward, because *he,* the experienced one, was supposed to be teaching *her.* It didn't make sense, except that maybe this was his way of making her feel comfortable. She didn't feel the least threatened. He didn't rush at her. He let her show him when she was ready for the next step.

"How on the mouth?" she whispered.

His eyes fell to her lips. *"Cara,"* he murmured. "I don't think I can…" He seemed to have trouble finishing his thought.

"You don't think you can what?" she asked.

He said nothing more for a long while, then it was as if he was speaking only to himself. "Can any man resist such a pretty invitation?" And his fingers left the champagne flute he'd held, then he took hers and placed it beside his on the countertop. Gripping her upper arms he brought her body flush with his.

There was an urgency in his embrace. He pressed her head to his chest for a moment, breathed deeply. She heard his heart racing against her ear.

And all she could think was: This is wonderful! This must be how a man makes a woman feel close to him. Feel protected, even though he might be the only thing she needs protection from!

A second later, he bent over her and lifted her chin to bring her lips up to his. This time his kiss was less gentle. He moved his mouth over hers, coaxing her lips open. He tasted of musk and spice and a nutlike freshness. She wondered what flavors she held for him, if he liked the way she tasted. Or was he forcing himself to go through the motions because he'd promised he would?

A new pressure came from his hands as they slid around from behind her, and followed her ribs upward. His eyes glittered, suddenly hard chips of obsidian. Then she was leaning back against the counter, one of his hands moving to support her, the other roaming hotly over her chest and coming to rest on one breast.

He found her nipple through the fabric, rubbed across it, back and forth with the pad of his thumb, and a blaze of heat raced from the tips of her toes to the very back of her throat. A smoldering sensation radiated through her limbs before condensing in a pool of warmth below her belly.

"Oh my!" she gasped, blinking up at him. "What was *that?*"

He smiled at her. "So soon, *cara?*"

She shook her head and laughed. "You're saying that I— Really?"

"Let's try that again," he murmured huskily, fitting her more securely into his arms.

She had the feeling that this time, as he held her body against his, was for his benefit more than hers. Or perhaps it was his intention to allow her to feel how aroused he'd become. For, despite her lack of experience, there was no doubt what she felt pressing against the flat of her stomach—the rigid proof of a man's hunger.

Suddenly afraid, Maria started to pull away from him. Maybe she had asked for more than she could handle.

As soon as he sensed tension in her body, Antonio leaned back and looked down at her. "What is it, *cara?*" His voice was hoarse, strained.

"I'm not sure I can do this."

"I moved too quickly for you. There should have been more time."

"No," she assured him, "it's not that."

She touched his cheek with trembling fingertips and gazed up into his eyes. Beneath the desire reflected in them was a layer of pain she hadn't noticed before, could only wonder at its source.

"I just thought when you showed me how a man made love, it would be more like a—" She struggled with words. "Well, more like one of my college professors lecturing me. You know, standard anatomy stuff."

"You would prefer that?"

She didn't even have to think about it. "No! But it might feel safer, if you can understand."

"You're afraid of me?"

"Afraid of something." A nervous laugh escaped her lips. "I'm not sure whether it's you or something I might find out about myself that I wouldn't like."

He observed her for a moment then picked up her glass

and brought it to her lips, and she obediently sipped. "Do you see what you just did?" he asked.

"I took a drink."

"Exactly. I offered you something. You decided whether or not you wished to accept, then you tasted."

"So?"

"This is how it should be between a man and a woman." His voice sounded richly musical; it mesmerized her. "The man offers the woman something new and, hopefully, delicious to taste, to see if she enjoys it. If she doesn't, she simply tells him, and he will stop and try something else. If she decides she cannot indulge at all, one word from her ends it."

She smiled at him, charmed by the ease with which he explained an act that had always seemed so confusing and risky to her. Perhaps that was one reason she'd saved herself for a husband. That fear every woman knew in her immortal soul. The terror that the person she trusted with her body might abuse the power he held over her, and she'd be physically as well as emotionally hurt.

But Antonio had already proven he could control whatever urges might assail him. Still she had so many questions. She drummed her freshly polished nails on the countertop. "This stopping whenever the woman says so. Is it at times, for a man, a bit…uncomfortable?"

He exploded in a full-bodied, ripe laugh. His eyes dancing with humor, he released her. "Dear lady, you have no idea."

"Then why—"

Touching two wide fingers across her lips, he silenced them. "Because it is only right. Because making love can't be perfect unless both man and woman are relaxed, trust each other, and seek to please their partner as much as they want pleasure for themselves."

Maria reached for her glass and, taking a sip of champagne, thought about this for a moment. Before she knew it, when she tipped up the stem nothing more came out. She set the glass down firmly. When she looked up out of a haze of pleasant anticipation, Antonio was putting on his coat.

"Where are you going?"

"Back to my hotel."

"Why? Oh, please stay! Really," she begged. "I *want* you to stay."

"If I do," he said, "I might not be able to follow my own advice. Do you understand?"

"Stay," she said. Maria opened her arms to him.

It took Antonio a moment to decide. "No more talking." He removed his coat and flung it across a chair as he strode across the room toward her. "I will show you. Remember what I said, though. Just a word from you, and I will stop. I will protect your virginity. That we will not jeopardize. It is as precious as you, *cara.*"

Antonio had already admitted to himself that he must be insane. This was a dangerous game, and all in the name of what? Educating a naive young woman? Hardly. He was gratifying his own needs. Needs that hadn't been satisfied in two agonizing years.

Tonight he felt alive!

Tonight he was reacting to a woman with a fierce lust that told him he'd returned from hell. At least, temporarily. Maria's sweet innocence, her healthy, glowing face and trusting gaze beckoned to him, drawing him out of the darkness. Being with her these two days had been like swimming up through the ocean's suffocating depths toward the light, to take his first real breath in years.

To think he'd offered to demonstrate the act of love. To think he'd had the audacity to promise such a thing to this young woman! Yet, by doing so he had been saved.

And who knew? It might last. If he kept his promise to her, he might wake tomorrow morning to fly back home as a whole man again.

Of course, he couldn't allow himself the ultimate pleasure, but he could revel in hers. Hadn't he already given her a taste of that delicious moment? Hadn't she already responded to him? And his hormones had gone gleefully along for the ride.

"Antonio? Is this all right?" Maria patted the couch cushion beside her.

"No," he said, startled to find she'd made her way across the room to the sofa while he'd been lost in his own thoughts. He strode to her, scooped her up into his arms, excited by the challenge at hand. He felt a thousand miraculous cravings, emotions he hadn't experienced for so very long. "We are going to your bed...to better simulate the most common setting. Where is—?"

"That door," she said, pointing.

He carried her toward the bedroom, dipping to turn the knob. When he stepped through, he stopped and scowled at the narrow mattress.

"What?" she asked. "It's a super twin."

"It will do," he said with determination. But what he wouldn't have given now for his sprawling feather bed back at the villa. He set her down on top of the bedspread then perched beside her.

"Should I take this off?" she asked, indicating the nearly transparent flow of silk over her body.

He shuddered at the delicious thought. "Shhh," he told her. "No talking now, unless it is to say that you like or do not like. Agreed?"

"*Si,*" she said, her eyes sparkling mischievously.

He slowly undressed her but did not remove his own clothing. He feared that doing so literally would be his undoing. If she so much as touched him, as aroused as he was, he would be unable to control himself.

When she lay naked before him, he began by caressing her breasts. They were small, lovely. When she lay on her back they melted against her body. He spread his palms over them, warming them, and the nipples rose to tight pink buds. He leaned down and kissed one, then the other.

She sighed.

"Is that a yes?" he asked.

She nodded.

Grinning, he chose one breast then opened his mouth over it and drew it gently between his teeth and softly nibbled. She arched her back beneath him. He suckled a little, filling his mouth with her delicate breast, running his tongue around and across her nipple.

Her fingers clutched at his shoulders, and he waited for the push that would signal him to stop. But the push never came.

Another yes.

He moved to her other breast and she began to squirm beneath him. Again he waited, but the sounds from her throat were deep, husky, redolent with pleasure. His own pleasure deepened. An engine throbbed within him.

His hands moved down the sides of her body, as his mouth trailed kisses down the center line of her stomach. He gripped her hips and pressed them up so that he could slide his palms beneath them and cup their fullness. His lips reached the soft pale fur between her legs, and he could sense her tensing, unsure of what he might do next. He was beginning to read her, and he felt sure he was treading the fine line that edged her trust.

He ached to run the tip of his tongue down the velvety trail between her soft thighs, to taste just once the sweet essence of her. But that was not something for Maria, the virgin. That would have to wait for another man who, if he treated her well, would be allowed to sample her luscious nectar.

His job was to start her in the right direction, show her the basics, and he would stick to that.

Slowly, painfully, he lifted his head until it was even with hers. He captured her eyes with his, held them, told her without words to concentrate upon all he was doing for her. She seemed to understand and didn't break their locked gaze.

Supporting her with one hand still behind her hips, he brought his other hand in front of her, dropping it down to her thighs. He smoothed his palm down one, then up slowly between them, lightly resting his hand over the soft curls of feminine fur.

He stayed there, not forcing, not probing. Just waiting for her answer to his unspoken question: *Will you let me in?*

She breathed between her lips and they quivered. He kissed her softly. Again the question.

She bit her bottom lip and looked at him for a long moment. Then, at last, she relaxed the muscles in her lovely legs, and her thighs parted just a few inches.

"Thank you," he whispered, just loud enough for her to hear him. And he slid his fingers up to touch her.

Gently, so gently, he stroked her. He watched her eyes grow distant, losing their focus, then slowly close.

Her eyelids fluttered.

Her breathing grew deeper, faster.

Her lips pressed together then pouted and opened on a soft gasp, then another. Her head fell back, and still he stroked her delicate moist center, flicking his finger over the tiny nubbin that guarded her precious womanhood, circling the tight orifice that would have delighted him to be the first to enter. But always moving away from it before temptation overwhelmed him.

Still, as he held her, pleasuring her, counting her climaxes as she writhed in his arms, then relaxed, only to tense again with mounting pleasure, his own needs became so urgent he couldn't swear that he'd be able to keep his promise. He could so very vividly imagine the heat of her closing around him, almost feel how welcoming that plunge into her would be.

He closed his eyes and held her tightly, moving his fingers deftly to grant her one final explosion of radiant delight. When he could no longer restrain the fire that seared his loins, he turned his face against her breasts with a groan, squeezed his eyes shut, and fought the raging beast within him that demanded satisfaction.

"Antonio?" Maria's voice came, whisper soft, from beneath him.

"*Si, cara?*" he asked weakly.

"I think...I think now I know what it feels like."

"Good."

"You can probably get off me now."

"*Si.*"

But it took every ounce of his remaining strength to do so. He looked at her—sparkling eyes, dazzling smile, pink cheeks vibrant with energy. How does she do it? he wondered, feeling as if he'd been knocked down by a Mack truck and dragged fifty feet...but liked it!

"So, is that sort of all of it? I mean, it was great," she clarified. "I never thought it would be so much fun. No. More than just fun. The feelings, they were marvelous! I've never felt so tingly all over, every inch of my body!"

He opened one eye to look at her warily. "There is more."

"Just as good, I hope."

"Even better." He gently traced the line of her jaw with one finger. Such a pity he'd promised not to... But he had, and he would stand by that pledge. "But much later. With your husband."

She looked at him with concern. "Are you all right? You look a little...that didn't bore you too much, did it? I mean, you didn't get much out of it for all that work. Maybe we could—"

Antonio pushed himself up off the bed with great effort. He could feel himself beginning to revive. He'd have to leave immediately, before his body showed her exactly how far from bored he'd become. Even now, gazing down at her naked on the bed, flushed with her first climaxes and the newness of lovemaking, he could barely control the rush of heat mounting again.

"I'm sorry, I can't stay any longer," he said lamely. "Early plane in the morning."

"I understand," she said softly. "You be careful getting back to your hotel. It's late." She blinked up at him, somehow managing to still look the innocent despite the ways she'd just allowed him to touch her.

On final impulse he reached for her hand, brought it to his lips, kissed her fingertips fervently. "Be careful with your heart, Maria," he whispered. "Wait for the right man."

"I will," she murmured, her eyes bright and alive and unforgettably beautiful.

Then he forced himself to turn away.

Four

The nightmare returned with a vengeance in the early morning hours. As so many times before, he relived the darkest day of his life. The day the *carabinieri* came to his door and told him that there had been an accident.

With the memory of past pain, came his body's usual reaction. Crying out in agony, Antonio rolled to his side in the hotel bed, clutching at his chest, helpless to fight off the spasms. All he could do was wait for it to pass.

He had been insane with grief for months. Only much later had he accepted that Anna was gone. She would never come back to him, to their little son, to the beautiful villa she'd so loved in the wild, rocky land of Apulia.

With her had gone all desire to love or to be loved. The sight of other women no longer moved him. He stopped dreaming of Anna coming to his bed. He never wished for a substitute lover. He ceased to feel like a man.

Antonio felt as dead to the world as she, at least in spirit. Breaking a cold sweat, he rolled again to stare at the white plaster swirls in the ceiling above the bed. The claw-ing ache in his chest that made it seem impossible to breathe wasn't imagined. It felt as if a bus had parked on his ribcage, then started spinning its huge wheels.

His physician had told him the attacks though intense, sometimes lasting for hours, were the result of severe mus-cle spasms caused by emotional stress. They would pass with time, he promised. Meanwhile, the pain seemed like small penance for having not gone with Anna that day in the car.

So now, he stared at the ceiling, lying flat on his back, waiting for the crushing pressure to recede. He tried to think of pleasant things to speed the process—his son; the groves of gnarled, rusty-leaved trees bearing a new crop of olives; a bountiful harvest; a fine glass of wine to accom-pany a rosemary-scented lamb roast.

None of the usual strategies worked today.

Then he thought of Maria.

Closing his eyes Antonio let himself drift back along the two days they'd shared. Days during which he'd thought of nothing but pleasing her. He felt the excitement return.

With the memory of her laugh and the vision of her pretty features, the bands of taut muscle across his chest began to unknot. He lay still for several more minutes, half expecting the tension to return. He remembered the way her flesh had yielded to his touch, how her eyes had wid-ened in astonishment and delight the first time she'd cli-maxed.

He began to breathe without discomfort.

After another ten minutes, the pain was completely gone. Antonio sat up in bed and frowned.

This was both good and bad, this power the American woman had over him. Good that the pain left, enabling him to function again. Bad because he had bid her farewell and expected never to see her again.

She had affected him deeply despite his vow to protect

himself from feeling more for any woman than *virilita* dictated. For the first time since his great loss, he felt like himself again. A man. Capable of great passion—for his land, his crops, for his son and even for women.

But he feared as much as welcomed these sensations. What if he found a way to keep Maria physically close to him and, as unlikely as it now seemed, she should become emotionally important to him? He could never survive the anguish of losing another so close to him.

Love was a curse!

But perhaps he might limit his investment in this woman, just as he would in all others. He might steer himself back through the motions of being a man, to satisfy the urges he'd felt with Maria last night. That was very different from love. That was a simple physical act.

Not love…lust! A smile gently tugged at the corners of his lips as he stood up and walked toward the bathroom. He was definitely in a sweet state of lust for Maria McPherson. A situation his body seemed only too eager to prolong.

But, he thought, if he left the U.S. and never saw Maria again, would he ever recapture these feelings with another woman? Ever be able to breathe without pain? To smile and laugh again? To find pleasure in a woman's body.

He had no choice but to return to Carovigno. This left only one option.

He must find a way to bring Maria back with him to Italy, at least temporarily.

Maria awoke feeling like a new woman. *This* was what all the big fuss is about!

Sex is a wonderful thing! she mused cheerfully.

It wasn't messy or embarrassing, painful or dirty-feeling. At least it hadn't seemed so with Antonio. She sat up in bed, energized, stifling a self-satisfied giggle. Feeling just a smidge wicked as she mused that she wouldn't mind ''learning'' all over again with him!

There was only one problem with that, aside from the fact she might have to stop fooling herself by insisting she was saving herself for her husband-to-be. Antonio had returned to Italy.

Carovigno, he'd said. A very small town in a remote part of southern Italy, which was a good-sized country. Geographically, she couldn't even picture where the place might be. Naples was the only southern Italian city she was familiar with.

Sad at the thought, Maria sulked for another twenty minutes then tossed back the sheets and marched herself into the bathroom, unwilling to let any man ruin her weekend. Weekends were golden when every workday was filled with tension.

She would go shopping. According to her neighbor, Sarah Brady, an expert on the subject, the perfect remedy for forgetting a man was a serious day's bargain hunting.

Maria drove to the mall and visited her favorite department stores and outlet shops, but none of them seemed very interesting after the places Antonio had taken her.

As the day moved along, all she could think about was *him*. Sure, they'd been together less than forty-eight hours, but she'd loved every minute of his exciting companionship. It was more than that. She felt as if they'd connected in a special way, although she couldn't define what that might be.

On a whim, she drove into Georgetown to the pottery shop he had taken her to, and spent over an hour admiring the beautiful terra-cotta and hand-painted porcelain. But of course she bought nothing. The prices were as high as she remembered.

Still, it was lovely to recall how delightful it had been when he had stood there beside her. She bought herself a small Caesar salad for lunch at a restaurant that had just opened its sidewalk café on that early spring day. She told herself it was in honor of Antonio and Italy.

Sarah was stepping from the apartment building's entrance as Maria locked her car. She grinned when she saw Maria coming.

"What's gotten you into such a great mood?" Maria asked.

"I'm just wondering how I can get a package like yours delivered," her neighbor said, laughing as she tossed back a flow of red curls over her shoulders.

Maria frowned, confused. "What package?" She hadn't ordered anything.

"The one waiting outside your door." Sarah moved off, walking backward down the sidewalk, smiling slyly, swinging her purse in great, happy loops. "Looks yummy!"

Maria took the elevator up, stepped off at the eighth floor, preoccupied with thoughts of the mysterious package...and let out a yip of surprise. "Antonio! What are you doing here?"

"Waiting for you. I knew of no other way to find you on the weekend. Your neighbor said she expected you wouldn't be much longer."

Maria's heart raced in her chest. She fumbled with her purse, dug out her keys, somehow managed the lock. "Well, come in. Did your flight get cancelled?"

He stepped up close behind her. His body radiated heat, and she caught a keen sensation of reined-in tension. When she turned around, he still hadn't answered her, and his expression looked strained. She dropped purse and keys on the coffee table.

"What's wrong?" she asked.

"Nothing is wrong," his deep baritone assured her, although she didn't believe it. He was looking around the room distractedly.

"Then why aren't you on your plane back to Italy?"

He swung around and observed her with a deceptively lazy smile. "I had a wonderful idea, Maria."

"You did?" she asked suspiciously.

Had he returned to *teach* her more? Part of her thrilled at the possibility. Another was instinctively wary. She had never intended to start an affair with him.

Or had she? Subconsciously, of course. That thought troubled her.

"Listen," she began, a little breathlessly, "I like you an awful lot, Antonio. But I never meant to take lovers before I married. I thought you understood that."

"I do," he assured her. "This has nothing to do with a sexual relationship."

"It doesn't?"

She was at a loss. What did he see in her besides a possible pillow partner?

"This is business," he stated solemnly.

She blinked up at him, waiting. "Business?"

"*Si.* I have told you about my family's *oliveti,* our groves, and the factory where we produce our *olio.*"

"Yes. But I don't see what they have to do with me. I have no experience with agriculture or manufacturing of any kind. I have the proverbial black thumb. No plant is safe in my apartment."

"That's not why I need you, Maria."

Something in his solemn tone and steady gaze made her even more wary. Was it her imagination, or did the words "need you" resound with multiple meanings.

Antonio took her hands and drew her down with him onto her couch. "Several years ago, I decided to introduce *Boniface Olio d'Oliva* to the American public. But I haven't yet found a way to guarantee success. It's a risky venture." He took a breath, his eyes bright. "I want you to design a marketing strategy for me. After all, you are in public relations, you are an American. You know what sells in this country and how to approach the public effectively."

Maria squinted at him, yanked her hands out from under his. "This seems rather sudden. Why didn't you mention such a possibility before?"

"Because it only occurred to me this morning." His expression seemed open, yet she couldn't help wondering if he was being totally honest with her.

"So I would be working for you?"

"For the company. I am chief operating officer and president. So, yes, in actuality, for me."

She felt suddenly hot, irritated and more than a little angry. Was he trying to manipulate her? Trick her? "You expect me to give up my job in this country, with all of my benefits—"

He interrupted. "I will make sure you are paid well. Here—" He pulled a piece of paper out of his hip pocket and unfolded it on the coffee table in front of her. She picked it up. "I called an associate here in Washington and asked him what the average salary would be for someone in your current position. Then I doubled it to make relocating worth your while."

"This much?" she gasped.

"Then I've guessed appropriately." He nodded, looking satisfied. "I want you to feel you are taking a step up in your career. The benefits you are leaving, I will match. I promise, you won't lose anything by accepting this offer."

She might be young, and still relatively inexperienced, but she wasn't totally naive to the ways of men in power. "And what would my duties be in addition to developing a marketing plan for your company?"

To his credit, Antonio didn't pretend not to understand what she was hinting at.

"I realize I can't expect you to become my mistress as part of this business arrangement. In the times of the Medicis, this would have been acceptable. In this new millennium, women can't be bought in this way." He looked down at her from beneath lowered lids, and the hunger she saw there was real and raw but, for the present, contained. "As disappointing as that might be to some men, including me."

A warm something curled low inside her stomach. She felt herself blush.

"I will have to let you determine the direction of our personal relationship. No matter what you decide, I will respect your professional advice and use it. I will also enjoy watching you color my life with your enthusiasm and joy."

He took her fingertips lightly, kissed them. "If it's your wish to keep our relationship strictly professional, I'll understand and respect that decision." He took the paper from her and laid it on the table so that he could take her other hand too. "I probably won't like it, but I'll live with it, *cara*."

She was too shocked to remain angry. "You actually find me that appealing? I mean, with all the women in your own country and other places you must travel…" She shook her head. "I don't understand."

"I'm attracted to you, but it's more than that. I find it easy to be with you, Maria, unlike with other women. I believe we could be very close friends. But I understand that you have other plans for your future, and I won't force the issue while you're my employee. If you wish to pursue your original dreams after fulfilling your business obligations to me, I'll not stop you from leaving."

She nodded, her throat feeling hot and tight. For several seconds, she couldn't swallow. Couldn't think.

Why did it matter that they wouldn't be together in the way she'd always imagined being with a man? Why did marriage mean so very much to her? How many women would toss aside all inhibitions for a lover like Antonio? Her head and heart felt awash with questions, emotions, and no answers at all.

"Come to Italy," Antonio whispered. "Come work for me. Promise to stay for at least six months to get my product off to a good start in the States. It will be hard work and long hours. But if you do this for me, you will receive a generous salary, a private suite on the estate, as many of your meals as you'd like prepared for you, even time off to travel."

Maria knew there were even more benefits than these. With the experience she would gain working for Boniface Olive Oil, she could reenter the U.S. job market, impressive credentials hot in her little fist. Any advertising or PR firm in the country would welcome her, and at a much higher position than as a fledgling associate.

He had offered her the stuff of dreams.

Maria was tempted to accept immediately. But she was also terrified. A sensually charged atmosphere had gripped them from the moment they met. No matter what Antonio promised, she feared the intimacy that being on his turf would assure.

"What happens," she asked slowly, "once we're working side by side every day? What happens if you make demands on me, or I am tempted to forget my promises to myself?"

He nodded. "Fair questions."

"I don't want to be put in the classic position—the secretary being chased around a desk."

"And are you more worried that I would catch you? Or that I might never give chase?" He was toying with her now.

"Antonio!"

"I'm sorry." He smiled. "I couldn't help myself. Please believe my word is good. I've already proven that once. Do you remember, Maria?"

Oh, she most certainly did remember. She recalled vividly every single move he'd made, every intimate, delicious sensation that had raced through her body at his experienced touch. And he'd kept his word then, stopping short of entering her, though it had obviously cost him.

"You have to understand," she tried to explain. "If I'm with you, romantically, I won't be available to Mr. Right, should he come along. I must guard my heart."

He nodded. "I accept this much. I won't expect more of you than you can give me—either professionally or in other ways." His smile seemed genuine, if still playful. "So what is your answer?"

She closed her eyes, hoping for a quick, sure answer. But nothing seemed clear to her. "I need a little time. I can't make such a big decision on the spot."

He sighed, looking troubled. "I need to return as soon as possible to take care of my affairs at home." He took a card from his wallet and handed it to her. "Take a few days. A week or two if necessary. Then call me with your answer. I promise, you won't regret coming, Maria. Be brave." He kissed the top of her head, gently. "Take risks; life is short."

Five

Take risks. Those were the words he'd left her with.

But risks weren't something she was accustomed to taking. Her favorite ice cream flavor was vanilla. Her chosen ride at the county fair was the merry-go-round. She hated roller coasters. When she selected a college, she started out at the local community college, so that she could still live at home, then moved to University of Connecticut because there was a campus still an easy bus ride away.

Easy, simple, safe choices were for her.

In a way, her career had been safe too. Although PR and advertising might seem high-profile jobs to some people, this had been the career of her best girlfriend's father. She had observed him with avid interest all of her growing years, and he had been a mentor to her.

Leaving the cities and country she'd grown up in, to move to a foreign land did not seem safe…or natural…or anything but terrifying. Yet something drew her along the path toward making that move. And at the end of three weeks she had quit her job, given notice that she was vacating her apartment, said farewell to Sarah and her other neighbors, and put her furniture in storage.

As Maria changed planes in Rome, from the sleek, silver Alitalia that had carried her eight hours across the Atlantic to the smaller prop job that would make the short flight to Brindisi on the southeastern coast of Italy, she was amazed that she'd severed nearly all ties with her past. It was so unlike her.

Cautious Maria. Bashful Maria.

But Antonio's words, more than anything else, had haunted her. There was more.

There was the memory of his touch. The irrefutable, compelling need to be close to him again. Despite her knowledge that he could never be *the one,* the important man in her life, she felt bound to follow him. To what end, she had no idea.

And so she stepped on the second plane, and sat watching out the window as the Apulian landscape came into view beneath her. The jade green of the Adriatic, tipped with white caps, sped beneath the plane's fuselage. A pale strip of sand and rock edged the shore, then the land rose sharply sometimes in jagged cliffs, sometimes in wedding-cake tiers of pastel villas, until it flattened out into rocky fields.

Here and there were villages and towns, many crested by what appeared to be the ruins of an ancient castle. Some structures appeared more sound than others. Cars parked nearby indicating they might even be inhabited.

They flew lower still. Between towns were rough fields growing what might be wheat or gray-green artichoke plants. The staked vines, she guessed, were varieties of wine grapes. Vast groves, at various stages of budding out and flowering, appeared to be the olive and almond trees she'd read so much about. Lemons, so immense and sunshine bright she could see them from the air, hung in profusion from the branches of still other trees.

Her heart raced with anticipation. One of those groves might be Antonio's, and one of those romantic, stucco villas below might be her home for the next six months. Such a daring adventure for herself she never could have imagined.

In Brindisi, the passengers used a metal staircase to disembark from the plane. Luggage was unloaded by hand from the compartment below the passenger seating and sorted onto carts. She spotted her bags and was about to reach for them when a hand gently moved her aside.

"I'll take them for you."

She turned, already waving off the porter whose services she didn't want to have to pay for. Antonio stood smiling down at her.

"Welcome to Italy," he said. "These are yours?"

"Yes," she said, her heart pulsing in her throat. "I didn't realize you'd be meeting me." He had sent her instructions to give the taxi driver on reaching Brindisi.

"I had spare time. There was no reason I shouldn't pick you up. Were your flights pleasant?"

"The first was very long, but I slept some."

"Good. You'll have time to rest at the house before we start work. Then I can give you a tour of the property including the groves."

"I'm not tired at all," she said. Which wasn't entirely true. But she was running on nervous energy now.

And, she thought, the sooner she became familiar with the groves, factory and house where she'd be living, the sooner she'd be able to start in earnest the work Antonio was paying her so well to do.

"Fine. We'll take your luggage to your suite by way of the garden, then walk the groves. The factory can wait for another day."

Maria had understood that Antonio was wealthy and

owned a sizable estate that had been in his family for generations. But until she actually arrived in Carovigno, she couldn't have comprehended how grand his lifestyle was in comparison to any she'd known.

As they walked the grounds, he described the estate, located a half mile from the center of the village. "My family's home is called a *masseria fortificata,* a fortified farm, originally built in the sixteenth century. The high stone walls once protected the noble residence, barns, sheds and laborers' cottages against highway robbers and pirates, who sometimes worked their way inland a few miles to raid wealthy landholders."

The main house was a two-storied villa of cream stucco. Deep green shutters framed generous windows, shielded from the intense Italian sun by modern retractable metal blinds. The roof was flat, as were most in the area. The buildings reminded her of photographs of Middle-Eastern architecture she'd seen in National Geographic magazines.

"If I remember my history," she said as they worked their way through the garden, "this part of the peninsula changed hands many times over the centuries."

"Another reason for building castles and little fortresses," he commented with a nod. "The ancient Greeks defeated the indigenous people, and were in turn defeated by the Romans. Saracens raided the shoreline repeatedly. For a time this area was under the protection of the Holy Roman Empire and, eventually, individual nobles."

"But even they were always battling each other for territory," she added.

He smiled appreciatively. "You know your history. Good. Maybe it will come in handy as you plan our American launch."

"It might at that," she agreed, glad she'd crammed like a high school student on the long flight.

She could see how the appealing architecture, art, agriculture and foods of the region reflected a rich mixture of ethnic influences. And Apulia was such a little known or understood area, compared to more popular tourist destinations like Rome and Venice. Perhaps this was grist for her advertising mill?

Her suite of rooms was on the second floor, and included a balcony overlooking the lush Mediterranean garden they'd just walked through. Roses were in full bloom, although it was only April. Portulaca blossomed in a profusion of summery hues, and azalea, lemon trees and hibiscus perfumed the air. Although the sea wasn't visible from the estate, the air was scented delicately with its salt.

"This is a beautiful place," she murmured, breathing deeply of the fragrant air.

"I hope you will be comfortable here, for the time you stay with us." Antonio had moved up close behind her shoulder. "The *masseria* was originally built by my family, then enlarged, rebuilt and modernized throughout the centuries until it has arrived at its present design.

"There are still catacombs beneath one wing of the house. Used as hiding places when invaders appeared. And those pillars you see at the far end of the garden date back to Imperial Roman times, before the house was built. Beneath the fountains there is brick work attributed to early Etruscan civilization."

This royal family, she thought, has roots! In her own country, only the lucky could trace their family back a few hundred years. Here, time was measured in millennia.

Maria intentionally stepped to one side before turning, so as not to bump into him. "I'll have to concentrate very hard to get any work done in these surroundings. They're exquisite, Antonio."

He smiled, looking pleased.

"Papa! Papa!" a little voice cried.

Waves of adoration mixed with pain crossed Antonio's face as he turned toward the door to the hallway. A toddler with curly, black hair and eyes as richly brown as his father's were blue, barreled through the door and toward the man. Antonio was down on one knee before the little boy reached him.

"*Ciao,* Michael. You have lost *Nonna* again?"

The little boy giggled and flung himself into his father's arms. *"Nonna, Nonna,"* he gurgled, obviously delighted with his recent escape.

"Michael, I'd like you to meet Signorina Maria. Maria, this is my son, Michael."

Maria crouched down to hold out a hand to the little boy. "It's very nice to meet you, Michael."

The child buried his face shyly in Antonio's shoulder.

"Oh, come now." Antonio laughed. "When have you not flirted with a beautiful lady?"

Maria stroked the back of one little hand with the tip of her finger. "It's all right. We'll get to know each other—"

Suddenly a stream of Italian issued from hall. Maria looked up to see the owner of the booming voice enter her rooms. A tall woman with gray hair and a loving smile stood in the doorway. "You little rascal, you don't run from your *nonna.*"

Maria's Italian was very limited, but she was able to understand a few simple phrases.

"He's fine," Antonio said. "I was just introducing him to Maria. Maria, this is my mother Genevra Teresa Boniface. Mama, please meet Maria McPherson of Washington, D.C."

Maria stood immediately and held out her hand. The older woman observed her coolly, nodded but did not clasp her hand. Had she committed a faux pas? Maria wondered. Perhaps women in Italy did not shake hands.

"You are to work for my son," she said solemnly in English.

"Yes. We're going to be working on a plan to introduce your olive oil to the United States."

Genevra shrugged. "I think we don't need to send it

anywhere. We're doing well without more business." She gave Maria a sharp look. "We were just fine as we were." Glancing meaningfully toward her son, she took the little boy from his arms and strode with purpose from the room.

A noticeable chill lingered in the air behind Genevra Boniface.

Antonio was silent. He gazed through the glass balcony doors, off into the distance.

"Did I say something wrong?" Maria asked.

"No. Nothing." But he didn't explain.

Maria walked to the doors, opened them and stepped outside. She breathed in the sweet air, waited. Antonio seemed deep in thought. After a while, he joined her on the balcony and took her hand in his.

"I'm sorry. That wasn't much of a welcome speech."

"She seems disturbed that I've come."

"No. She's afraid."

"Afraid of me?" Maria was shocked.

"I don't think she believes you've come here to work for me. I expect she thinks that you are my..." He hesitated.

"Your mistress?" She smiled and shook her head in disbelief.

"Yes. You see, she was very fond of Anna, my wife. My mother grew up here in Carovigno, with Anna's mother. They were dear friends, until the other woman passed away. Then I married her daughter, and we had Michael. My mother couldn't have been happier."

"Until your wife died in the accident."

"Yes. But even then she found a way to overcome her grief. She took care of Michael. He was just an infant then. She has been wonderful with him. And he is her world."

"But how would my coming here threaten her relationship with her grandson?"

"If you aren't a simple employee, if you are my mistress…or become my wife, you might take her *bambino* from her.''

Maria met his eyes. He was serious.

''I'll have to reassure her that I have no designs on you.'' She gnawed her bottom lip thoughtfully. ''And Michael is charming, a beautiful little boy. He's clearly attached to his grandmother. Can't she see that?''

He let out a wry laugh. ''Convincing my mother of anything she has her mind set against is no small task. She apparently has you pegged as a dangerous interloper. *Buona fortuna!*''

Maria sighed. She hadn't bargained on having to deal with family politics in addition to a challenging new job.

''Come,'' Antonio said, pulling her by the hand, ''let's go meet your new clients.''

''I thought you were my client.''

''The olives,'' he clarified. ''They are your real clientele. They produce the liquid gold we hope to bring to America.''

She went willingly with him. As soon as they left the steps that led down into the garden, he released her hand. She sensed that he didn't want his mother, or perhaps staff, to see them touching.

That was fine with her. If theirs was to be a professional relationship, they should get off on the right foot.

Yet she couldn't help feeling excited, just by being near him again. Antonio was a tall, strong, sensual man in the way he moved as much as in the way he looked. He made her think of heroes from novels she'd read as a teenager. Men with strength of will, men of honor.

Hadn't he been gentleman enough to apologize to her in person for his former valet's missed appointment? Hadn't he kept his word when she'd asked him to demonstrate the intimacies between a man and a woman? He was a unique and intriguing male. What woman wouldn't want to call him her own?

Yet, she reminded herself not for the first time, this simply wasn't possible. Not on her terms.

They walked through the garden, and she brushed her fingertips along the granular surface of the stones that appeared to be hundreds if not thousands of years old.

To think...thousands of years ago, another man and woman might have walked along this same wall. Another couple might have stopped to embrace and share dreams.

But she and Antonio were not, she reminded herself, a couple. Not in any sense of the word.

"What are you thinking?" he asked.

She jumped, startled by the question. "Possibilities for opening your ad campaign," she lied.

"And they are?"

Fortunately, she had already done some preliminary planning. "Since there are other Italian olive oil companies, as well as Greek and Spanish, vying for the American market, we need to come up with a unique hook. Something no one else has done before."

"And you have ideas?"

"Nothing firm yet. In the time before I left the States, I researched your competitors' ads—television, radio and print. A couple of them are very effective, and I wish we'd thought of them first." She sighed. "They have the kind of visual impact we're looking for."

"I see." He nodded and walked around a tuft of grass growing in the path.

Their arms brushed—his bare skin against her dress sleeve. A tingle zipped up to her shoulder and through her body. He didn't move away.

Abruptly, Antonio stopped at a gate. Beyond it was a field of olive trees, trunks and limbs twisted into bizarrely beautiful shapes. Under each, wrapped around the trunks on the ground, were yards and yards of what looked like white cheesecloth.

"What's that for?" she asked, pointing.

"To catch the fruit that drops prematurely from the trees. The cloth keeps it from bruising or rotting before we can retrieve it."

She nodded. "How is the fruit picked?"

"By hand, in the ancient way. Machines are used by some growers, but that can damage the olives. A few bruised or rotten fruit can spoil the flavor of an entire vat of oil."

She smiled at him. "You care very deeply about your product, don't you?"

"It is my life," he said solemnly.

She could see that. She could also see that the olives probably had saved his life after the death of his wife. If he hadn't had them, grief might have destroyed him. Without thinking what she was doing, Maria reached up and gently touched his face.

Antonio didn't move. Didn't react to the brush of her fingertips, except through his eyes. They blinked once, then again. Somehow, she couldn't remove her hand.

Her fingertips felt magnetized to the flesh of his jaw, lightly stubbled with new growth of his beard. She gently stroked down toward his chin, then let her fingers drop away. She started to step back.

"Don't!" His voice sounded brittle, hoarse.

She froze and held her breath. Seconds passed. Heartbeats.

Suddenly he seized her by the shoulders and hauled her against him. She looked up to see he'd closed his eyes. He lowered his head, and she was sure he was going to kiss her. She didn't try to move away.

His lips on hers were firm, demanding.

He pressed so hard against her mouth that she felt she might bruise, like his precious fruit. Maria gasped for breath, yet he didn't stop. He was like a starving man. Yet she sensed that what he needed from her was far more complex than sex.

Her arms came up around his neck. She clung to him, letting his kiss deepen and swell, filling her with her own needs. She felt the sun beating down on her shoulder blades, and the groves around them smelled of new, raw growth and hot soil and the sea that had brought both wealth and invaders.

And the musky, human scent of a man and a woman in heat.

One of his arms wrapped around her waist. The other hand clasped her bottom and pressed her hips against his muscled thighs. She felt his erection against the wall of her stomach.

Suddenly, he broke off the kiss and buried his mouth in her hair atop her head. Her body throbbed with unsatisfied desire. Her breasts pressed against his chest, and she knew he must feel them resting heavily against him.

"Ma-ria!" he ground out her name.

"Antonio, I don't know what to—"

"No! Say nothing. Just let me hold you a moment longer. Please."

She did as he asked. He held her, and she understood that he was holding something else too. His pain.

"I'm sorry," he said at last. "I don't know why I...I just needed to touch and be touched. To hold someone. I wanted to feel again what I had felt a long time ago."

So that was it. She was a surrogate for a dead wife. All at once, Maria felt hollow inside. Slowly, she pulled out of his arms.

"There's no need for apology," she said stiffly. "It must have been very difficult for you, these past years."

"Still, there's no excuse for this behavior. I didn't mean to kiss you, not here. Not without your consent."

She sighed. How could she admit to him that his kiss had affected her deeply, thrilled her, drove her toward begging for more from him?

"I think we'd better keep this on a professional level, as

we'd agreed," she said at last. "I can't do the job I've come to do and deal with this." She gestured at her disheveled dress.

"I know. I'm sorry if I forced myself on you. It won't happen again."

"Good," was the word she said.

But the ones she thought were, *Too bad*.

Six

"**D**on't worry," Antonio said. "I'll take Michael with me today." He held out his arms to his son and the little boy cheerfully flopped into them.

"But you have so much to do today." Signora Boniface winced and closed her eyes against another wave of pain. True, he did have work, and in the week since he'd made his promise to Maria, little of it had been done.

But as far back as Antonio could remember, his mother had suffered from migraine headaches. Even with the Imitrex, it would be an hour or more before she started to feel any relief. Until then, lying in a dark, silent room, was the best treatment. That wasn't possible with a rambunctious three-year-old.

"I'll take him with me to the fields this morning. If you're feeling better by noon, I can go to the factory then."

He'd have to call his plant manager and tell him he wouldn't be there as planned. It was disappointing and an inconvenience, but he didn't want to leave the child with one of the servants, who already had enough work. Besides, Michael was a shy child who wouldn't stay willingly with just anyone.

Genevra's little villa was set on the south edge of the gardens. This separate structure, as well as other buildings now renovated as living quarters for his staff and shelter for agricultural equipment, were all enclosed by the three-foot-thick walls, overgrown with ivy and tendrils of morning glory. A second nursery had been designed for her house after Anna's death, and that was where Michael spent most of his time.

After making sure his mother was as comfortable as possible, Antonio took Michael with him. They were rounding a tall, lush hedgerow when he ran into Maria. She treated him to no more than a polite business smile, and that stung him. But he told himself he only had himself to blame. He had put her in a difficult position.

"Buongiorno," he said.

Michael giggled and hid his face against his father's neck.

"Good morning to you both," Maria replied. "It's beautiful out here early in the morning. I thought I'd take a walk to clear my head before starting the workday." Her office was fully equipped and located within the suite of rooms allotted her in the main house. "Are you off to the factory now?"

Antonio shook his head. "Change of plans. Michael is spending at least part of the day with me."

"That's nice. A father-son day?"

"Yes, but not planned. My mother suffers from incapacitating migraines. When she is in the middle of one, she can't do much of anything. Caring for a child would be impossible."

"That's a shame," Maria said sincerely as she touched the rim of Michael's ear. "You are a shy little one, aren't you?" she purred.

The little boy snuck a peek at her.

"Do you think he'd stay with me for a few hours? I'm still just getting my thoughts together before sketching out ideas for our promotion."

Antonio considered this. He didn't want to request tasks of Maria that weren't part of her job description. But it would really help him out. "If you don't mind, that would be great," he agreed. "But I doubt he'll go with you."

"Hmm. Maybe we can find something Michael likes to do." Having been the neighborhood baby-sitter as a teenager, she'd become quite adept at handling moody little munchkins. "What are his favorite games or books?"

Antonio thought for a moment, surprised and embarrassed to realize he didn't know what his son liked to do. Since Anna's death, Genevra had taken full charge of the child, treating him as her own. A relief to him at first, as he'd been so crushed by his own pain he could barely remember how to breathe. But as time had passed, he'd gotten out of the habit of spending time with his son.

"Games? I'm afraid I don't know." A thought occurred to him. "But he seems to like being taken in his stroller to market. *Mercato*, Michael?" he asked the child.

The little boy squealed and started wriggling from his father's arms before Antonio could put him down.

"So that's the magic word," Maria laughed. "*Mercato!* Where is his stroller?"

As soon as Genevra's maid brought the colorful canvas-shaded vehicle out to the garden, Michael clambered into it on his own and started rocking back and forth, as if to get the engine started.

"Well, I guess we're going to market this morning," Maria said cheerfully. "Anything we should purchase while we're there?"

Antonio stared in amazement at his son, setting off so cheerfully with a virtual stranger. Or was it because it was Maria? Such a gentle, sweet woman. Like father, like son?

He was tempted to go along with them. It would be fun to spend some time with his child. And that would provide ample excuse for hanging out with Maria.

In the brief time she'd been at the *masseria,* they had talked frequently but been cautious about being alone together since the steamy episode in the garden. Despite her rejection of him as a lover—for reasons he fully understood—he still wanted her.

It was an aggravating but unalterable truth. He desired her. Somehow, he was going to have to find a way to deal with that impasse—either by changing her mind, or by quelling his hunger by other means.

He took several notes from his wallet—the equivalent of about a hundred American dollars—and handed them to her.

"I'm sure Sophia has more than enough food in the kitchen, but if anything special appeals to you, feel free. Or if you need anything at all for yourself," he added. "The local women are known for their hand-knitted sweaters, and there are all sorts of surprises in the stalls. Just be sure not to pay full price. You bargain for everything here."

"Thank you," she said, taking the money. "I'll get something for Michael, and maybe a treat for all of us too."

He nodded. She looked so beautiful with the morning sun warming her cheeks. Later, the day would grow warm and humid, but in the early morning the coolness of night still seeped from stone and stucco walls and cobbled streets.

He watched her walk away, chatting easily with Michael as she pushed along his carriage. The child seemed oblivious that a stranger was taking him away. An unexpected chill crept up his spine. It was the second time he'd had that thought. The child usually was bashful around strangers, but clearly there were ways of distracting him. Was this a danger he should worry about?

Antonio shook off the sensation of foreboding. Maria was with the child, and she was absolutely trustworthy.

Nothing would happen to Michael. And they made such an appealing pair. Even as he turned toward the black Ferrari and headed out for his factory, he wished he'd made up a threesome with them.

Maria strolled along narrow streets of Carovigno, the carriage bumping merrily over smooth cobbles that might have been set in medieval times. Most of the buildings through town were of stone or cement block, covered with plaster and painted white or pastel washes of color. Doors were massive wooden affairs, hinges and locks rusting with age but still offering substantial resistance.

She felt as if she'd stepped back in time.

Antonio had told her that Carovigno's market area was near the top of the hill, outside the castle walls. If she took any upward climbing street, she would run into it.

The journey up the steep streets wasn't easy, between the weight of the carriage and its occupant. By the time the ground leveled out, only narrow alleys seemed to remain, sometimes barely wide enough for a single tiny Fiat to squeeze through, or a donkey pulling a cart.

Suddenly, the path she'd taken opened out into a beautiful little piazza. Stalls had been erected to show off hand-painted pottery, woven tapestries and rugs, plastic ware and brilliant copper pots. Swaths of rainbow-hued cloth had been spread across the paving stones, then piled high with succulent oranges and huge lemons, brown almonds, field-ripe artichokes, olives, potatoes and greens.

The sight took her breath away.

Michael squealed with delight as she wheeled past a booth piled with fragrant breads, some twisted and sprinkled with sugar and fragrant anise.

"Time for your treat?" Maria asked him.

He bounced impatiently in his seat.

She pointed to the sugary pastries, and his eyes grew round. She purchased a small sack of the goodies and gave one to her shopping partner. He leaned back in his seat to suck and gnaw contentedly on the pastry twist.

She munched on one, too, and decided Michael had excellent taste.

They wheeled up and down the street, checking out seconds of American linens marked down to bargain prices she couldn't believe. Ceramic plates and bowls of reds and blues caught her eye. The atmosphere was carnival-like. And it only added to the adventure that she could understand just a few words of Italian.

She loved every minute of their adventure.

After purchasing several types of fruit then a pretty shawl to mail to Sarah, she turned around to head back down to the *masseria* but discovered a side street with several additional stalls. She stopped at the first, which offered European-sized leather sandals, and held up a pair alongside her right foot for comparison.

"You like, *signorina?*"

"They're very pretty," she said in Italian. "Is this about my size?"

The young, dark-eyed man observed her foot. "One smaller, I think, *signorina*. Marco, *trentasette!*" He held up the sandal for the other man to see the style.

A sullen-looking fellow, who might have been the vendor's brother from the similarity of their features, mumbled, *"Si, Frederico!"* and disappeared behind stacks of boxes.

A moment later he reappeared, holding up the shoes. He wore a long-sleeved green shirt and a black cap pushed back on his head, neither looking very clean.

"Grazie," she murmured politely, taking them from him. She slipped one on her right foot, aware that he was hovering close by. When she looked up he was staring at Michael.

"Che bel bambino!" he said, his eyes bright specks of interest.

The little boy looked up but didn't smile at the stranger. He busily attacked his pastry.

Marco, she thought belatedly. Wasn't that the name of the young man from the escort service whose place Antonio had taken? But then, it was a very common name.

"This is little Michael, no?" Marco asked. "So big he grows now. You work for *la famiglia* Boniface?"

"In a way. You know them?" she asked.

"*Si,* very well. Everyone in town knows *Il Principe.* His is a very rich family, no?"

"*Basta,* Marco!" Frederico snapped, then added in English. "I will take care of the pretty lady."

But Marco stood his ground. He reached out and stroked Michael's soft head. Maria automatically moved closer, as if to protect the child.

Marco smiled at her. "Such a sweet child. La Signora Boniface is blessed indeed. Is she not, brother?"

"*Si,* most blessed," the vendor said with little enthusiasm. "Now go back to sorting those shoes."

"And *Il Principe,* he is back from his travels now?" Marco asked, ignoring his brother.

"Yes, he's back," she answered then turned to the other man. "*Quanto costa?*" she asked, holding up the sandals.

The vendor quoted her a sum in Euros. She offered the vendor a quarter less than his asking price.

"They are yours," Frederico said immediately, making her think she still had paid too dearly for the shoes.

But she was anxious to return to the security of the estate.

"La Signora—she is well these days?" Marco asked as she handed her money to his brother.

"Yes, fine," she said automatically, unwilling to give out family information to strangers.

"And the *bambino,* she still cares for him in her own villa?"

"I'm really in a hurry," she said, taking her change. "Thank you, we have to be going."

"We will very much look forward to seeing you again soon," Marco called after her cheerfully. "Very soon, *signorina.*"

She walked quickly, sensing he was watching her. Warning prickles danced up her spine. She touched the top of Michael's head nervously, as if to reassure herself that he was all right. She couldn't have said why she'd been so unnerved by the two men. Two more blocks down the road, she stopped to buy oranges from a woman who sat on the curb.

"The men selling shoes up the street," Maria asked in what she hoped was understandable Italian after her purchase was complete. "Do you know them?"

"*Si,*" the woman said, "*i fratelli Serilo. Marco e Frederico.*"

Yes! She remembered now. Serilo had been the name Antonio had mentioned. Marco Serilo. He'd been Antonio's valet, the one he'd fired then flown to New York to stop from using his name.

There had been something vaguely unsettling about the man's interest in the family. Even the brother had seemed unnerved by his pressing for information.

Maria rushed down the hill and didn't stop to catch her breath until she was inside the masseria's formidable gate.

"What is it, Maria?" Antonio asked.

As soon as she returned to the house she'd asked one of the servants to call Antonio at the factory, but somehow the message had gotten mixed up. Instead of just coming to the phone, he'd rushed back to the villa.

"Is something wrong with Michael? My mother?"

"They're both fine," she reassured him.

Michael had decided she was worthy of his attention since she'd taken him for a spin that morning. He was cuddled up beside her on the couch in her suite by the time Antonio rushed in. "Maybe I'm just imagining trouble where there is none. But I thought you ought to know that I ran into Marco Serilo at the market."

"Marco? What was he doing there?"

"Working for his brother, apparently. They were selling shoes."

"The family has had stalls in Carovigno, San Vito, and Ostuni for many years. But Marco would have nothing to do with them while he worked for me. He felt hawking footwear was beneath him."

"He certainly didn't look very happy today."

Antonio let out a dry laugh. "I shouldn't be surprised." He frowned and studied her expression. "Something frightened you?"

"I'm not sure frightened is the word. More like concerned me. He was asking a lot of questions about you, your mother, the family in general. It just seemed odd."

"Maybe he was curious to see if anything had changed since he left. He wasn't a bad valet. Very conscientious in many ways, but he had slippery fingers. Stole from everyone in the house, even though it was small amounts."

"You don't think he might try to get back at you for firing him? Or for spoiling the good thing he had going in America?"

Antonio thought for a moment. "I grew up with the Serilo boys, and many others in this town. Our parents all grew up in Carovigno. If one of us boys stepped out of line, there was always an adult to pinch an ear and drag us home. There may be jealousies and hard feelings at times, as in any family, but I expect the Serilos are harmless. If Marco means to make trouble, it will be of the mischievous variety." He touched Maria's arm reassuringly.

She rested her cheek against the little boy's head and rocked him. Something still didn't feel right to her. "I suppose you're right," she murmured. "You know them."

He held out his hands to his son, but Michael crawled into Maria's lap and turned his rosy cheek against Maria's chest. His preference, for the moment, was clear.

Antonio laughed at him. "I don't blame you a bit, little man. If she let me nuzzle her breasts like that, nothing in the world would make me move."

Maria felt her cheeks go hot.

Antonio laughed again then, his eyes softening as he watched woman and child, he said, "All right. Perhaps caution is in order. It won't hurt to keep an eye on the boys. I'll have a couple of my men watch Marco and Frederico. If they're up to anything, we'll soon know. Does that make you feel better?"

"Much." Maria looked down at Michael, his breathing had slowed and his eyes were shut. "I think he's asleep."

"If we put him down in his bed in the nursery, he'll probably sleep for an hour or two. We'll have enough time for lunch."

"All right," she agreed. "But it will be a working lunch. I have a few ideas about your ad campaign to run past you."

They ate on the stone patio overlooking the gardens while one of the maids kept an eye on Michael as he slept. La Signora still hadn't left her villa, so it was just the two of them.

They lunched on artichokes stuffed with creamy goat cheese and herbs, thick slices of ripe tomatoes drizzled in fragrant first-press olive oil with a delicate flavor then sprinkled with fresh basil, and still-warm bread baked that day in the outdoor stone oven in the courtyard. Antonio selected a local white wine.

Maria felt sure she had been transported directly to heaven. Only a few months earlier, she never would have guessed she'd be living in Italy, in a palatial villa above the Adriatic, consuming Mediterranean delicacies.

Life, she thought, sure does dish up surprises.

Antonio looked up at the sky when the first drop of rain fell on the back of his hand. "We'd better move inside."

She studied the fluffy clouds above them. "Maybe it's just a freak drop or two. It's a shame to go in when it's such a lovely day. The food tastes so much better out here in the open air."

He knew how quickly storms came up over the Adriatic, but smiled indulgently at her. "As you wish."

Minutes later, the sky opened up. With a squeal, Maria grabbed her plate and wineglass, dashed through a rear doorway into the main house. Antonio ducked inside after her, and they stood laughing and gasping for breath in his private office, their clothing already soaked through. She glared at the sheets of gray water washing the landscape.

"You did warn me," she admitted. "I should have listened."

"You should have. I have a very good reputation for knowing what's best."

"When it comes to the weather," she added.

"Often other things as well."

"Really?" She lifted a skeptical eyebrow. "Like what?"

She'd given him such a tempting opening. "Like when the olives will reach their peak ripeness, what color tie to wear with a suit, and whether or not you should sleep with me." He reached behind the door for a towel and started drying her shoulders and hair.

When he dared steal a peek at her expression, she was no longer smiling. "I was only joking," he said quickly.

She wasn't having any of it. Her voice was clipped. "I thought we'd settled this."

He shrugged. There was little use in trying to cover up now. "I've changed my mind. I believe your education should be extended."

"Maybe I don't need a doctorate to function as a wife. *Maybe* my little bachelor's degree will do." She looked up at him through long, dark lashes, and he wanted to grab her there and then.

"One can never be too well-prepared," he countered, smoothing the damp towel down her throat to her chest. He patted the front of her sweater.

She stared up at him, her mouth pursed thoughtfully. Her eyes calculating possibilities.

"Look," he said, "I stand by my promise not to force myself on you. And I truly do respect your plan to wait for marriage to lose your virginity. Technically, that is."

"You're playing with semantics," she whispered, "as well as with my heart."

He stiffened. "Hearts have nothing to do with this, Maria. We're two healthy adults who have every right to enjoy ourselves and each other. The fact that we're not in love and don't intend to marry shouldn't stop us from sharing a little pleasure."

She shook her head but her hand lifted to touch his cheek. Her smile was shaky. "More than a *little* pleasure, if I remember correctly." Drawing her hand away quickly, she snapped the towel out of his grasp. "But I don't see how we can pretend that what we did or what you propose to do isn't making love."

"It's sex," he said. "Nothing more or less."

Her gaze dropped away from his. "Maybe for a man. But a woman can't help bonding emotionally with her partner. At least, that's what I've read."

"You read too much."

He took the towel from her, tossed it aside, wrapped an arm around her waist and hauled her to him.

Antonio's lips crushed down over hers before she could draw a breath. The muscles in her legs weakened, wobbled. A fiery sensation crept up from her chest to her throat and face. As the world careened and whirled out of focus, his kiss deepened.

At last she pulled back, their lips parting. "I do read too much," she whispered breathlessly.

"But you have a point," he admitted, the desire still there, still struggling to take control and push him over the edge. "Maybe this attraction between us is more complex than—" He groaned in frustration. "I just don't know."

Antonio ached to ignore both his own and her inhibitions. To take her the way he wanted to take her. Brazenly. Completely. Sinking deep within her body. Her flesh perfectly, completely encasing him. He was ready. And it had been an eternity since he'd felt this way.

Dio! He wanted her. But Maria had every right to deny him her body. He hadn't passed the point of reason.

Nevertheless, masculine hormones were driving hard within him and he felt compelled to try again. "I think it's very possible for two people to become attached without being in love."

"Attached?" she repeated, looking at him as if he were newly discovered species. "That's a pretty vague word for something that feels this passionate."

Passion?

Yes, he supposed this was true passion. But passion wasn't a synonym for love in his dictionary.

Still, he had thought of nothing but her from the moment they'd met. He touched a finger to the tip of her nose, then to the center of her solemnly pursed lips.

"Maria, you are an infuriating, lovely young woman. I can't imagine why I haven't backed you against that wall and made you beg for me."

She choked on a laugh. "Me, beg? Fat chance."

He growled at her playfully. "Is that my bluff I hear being called?"

She shrugged and looked away, feigning indifference, although he could feel her trembling. "Take it as you like. But we're not consummating this relationship of ours, whatever it might be."

"Very well then. Do you remember what I told you in your own country, about trying things and your ability to choose?"

She slanted him a cautious look. "I remember."

"Good. Then how about this?"

He swept both hands up the sides of her body from hips to shoulders, then brought them around in front of her and pressed his palms over her breasts. She backed up a step, then another, hit the wall.

"Nowhere to go," he whispered huskily. "Do I hear a stop yet?"

She shook her head, seemed unable to speak. Her eyes were wide as she watched him unbutton her blouse. Slipping a hand inside her bra he gently cupped one breast, then began to tease the nipple with the field-roughened pad of his thumb. Her head dropped back against the wall and she shut her eyes.

He watched her mouth, waiting for the refusal he expected. But when she parted her lips only a long breath came out.

He felt mad with desire, still hated himself for seducing her. For there was no other word for what he was doing at this moment. He wanted her. He wanted her desperately and would have done nearly anything to coax her to toss away all her inhibitions and welcome him into her body.

Touching her this way, the last of his reason left. He brought his head down to her breast and, moving his hand to lift it gently toward him, he opened his mouth over the pure white mound of flesh cradled in his palm and sucked softly. His tongue circled her nipple, flicking at the hardening nubbin, bringing it to an even tighter peak.

He drew harder, suckling with a thirst that only left him wanting more. He moved to her other breast, treated it equally. He was aware of her body moving against his mouth, her hands sliding to the back of his head to press him harder against her. She shifted her hips against his thighs, hands to his butt...and held him there, against her body, keeping him from leaving even if he'd tried.

"I'm not...begging," she gasped.

He nearly laughed. "Then I will. Take me in your hand. Please...now." She started to comply, but wasn't fast enough for him.

He gripped her wrist, guided her down below his belt. Hastily, he undid the buckle, zipper and released himself. She cautiously laid her hand over his erection. Slowly she wrapped her fingers around him.

That nearly finished him.

The heat of her hand entrapping him brought him to the precipice. But he closed his eyes, concentrated, held back just a little longer.

Antonio reached up beneath her skirt, found the slim elastic edge of her panties, moved his hand underneath.

She tensed with anticipation.

He held his breath and waited.

She didn't tell him to stop. Instead she murmured barely coherent syllables that sounded inviting, intoxicating, urging him on. He moved a knuckle, back and forth, over the delicate button of flesh that guarded her virginity.

He would go no further unless she asked. This, he suspected, might be enough for her. She was climaxing even now, a continuous series of peaks that sent her writhing in his arms. If she would return the gift...perhaps that too would suffice.

For a time.

Perhaps they could continue to pleasure each other in this way without robbing her of her dream.

He felt her lean into his hand, rub against the hardness of his knuckle. As if she intuitively knew what to do next, she began to stroke him, running her soft fingers up and down his full length.

He shuddered with each stroke. Moaned.

Glorious...glorious! he thought. Close. So very close.

Shutting his eyes, he buried his face in the soft hollow at the base of her throat. Harder. Faster.

Maria let out a sharp, shudderingly sweet moan of ultimate satisfaction. Only then did he allow himself his own urgently sought release.

His body seized, muscles straining along the backs of his thighs, the flat of his stomach, his shoulders and arms. Every nerve raging, afire. His insides pulsing with ecstasy beyond anything he'd ever experienced before.

Seven

"**I**'m sorry."

The first words from his lips stunned, then stung her. Like twin lightning strikes, shattering the veils of warm bliss that had settled over her following Antonio's expert caresses.

"What?" Maria whispered dazedly, still pinned between his body and the office wall.

Antonio drew back from her and looked around the room as if seeing it for the first time. "I shouldn't have done that," he stated grimly.

Maria scowled at him. There she had been drifting in a lovely, sparkly haze of sexual fulfillment...and the man was telling her it had all been a big mistake?

She slid from between the hard of his body and hard of the wall, and stared at him. "You shouldn't have kissed me? Shouldn't have touched me, or asked me to make you—"

"Any of it. None of it," he muttered turning to walk

away from her. "I never meant to force you to have sex with me."

"Well," she cleared her throat and propped the heels of her hands on her hips, "you could have fooled me."

"Maria—"

"No, you're right," she snapped, drawing a deep breath, buttoning the front of her blouse. "It wasn't a seduction. I knew that I could ask you to stop. I didn't want you to stop. That's all there was to it."

"You're angry."

Damn straight I'm angry! she thought. Didn't she have every right?

She shrugged with too much emphasis. "So?"

He was shaking his head, mumbling to himself, busy tucking himself back into his pants. Despite her annoyance with him, she watched. Fascinated by the intricate male process of repositioning articles that females never had to bother with.

"I took advantage of you," he stated.

She wasn't going to let him feel sorry for her, if that's what he wanted. She had *liked* what they did—thrilled at touching him and being touched in ways she'd never imagined. She wouldn't play the victim and refused to allow his sudden attack of conscience take that away from her.

"You *thought* you took advantage of me," she corrected him stiffly. "Maybe having a fling is the real reason I came here. Maybe I've been using you. Had you thought about that?"

He winced. "I can't imagine, actually. Besides, you don't understand how close I came to—"

"Making love to me? *Going all the way?*" she taunted.

"Yes. That." He rolled his eyes, turned back to fully face her and gripped her arms with both hands. "It had been too long. I told you that. Warned you. Do you realize what that does to a man? He shuts down. Stops feeling."

She shook her head, not wanting to feel sympathy for

him now, while she was hurting. "It must have been painful," she allowed.

"It has been. But when I'm with you, when we are in the middle of our battle of wills, gripped by this compulsion...the pain goes away. All I think about is you, Maria. I feel whole again."

She felt her heart stop. Five seconds later, it started up again, and she found she could breathe.

He could have hit her with a hundred excuses for messing with her heart, her newly discovered sexual awareness, her womanhood...but this one worked. Without even trying, she had become the one woman he obsessed about. And the one who, at least in this way, made him happy.

"I like that," she whispered, telling herself even as she said the words that she shouldn't be so weak, shouldn't let him inside her soul like this.

He studied her expression. "That you have so much power over me?"

"No. That I can heal you." She smiled at him, brushed fingertips along his jaw, then pressed her hand over his heart. "I'm glad you can feel again, Antonio. No one should go through life without experiencing the joys life has to offer." Even if achieving that means trampling all over my life, she added silently.

"Learning to feel again has its disadvantages," he said with a wry grimace. "No matter how exciting it is to be with you, to show you ways to find pleasure with a man, I can't help wanting more of you."

"I don't know what to do about that," she murmured, dropping her hand to her side.

"You don't? I thought you were very sure."

"I am...or I was...I just don't know any more." She sighed. "It's a worthy dream, isn't it?"

"To marry and have children?" He nodded. "Very worthy, Maria. Very precious." He searched her eyes intently, and she could tell he was searching his own soul as well.

"But you can't blame me for wanting to possess you, if only for a few weeks or months. If I had my way, I'd keep you here for as long as you'd stay, Maria."

She stared up at him, terrified yet excited. He was saying that he wanted her as his mistress. He wanted her to be with him, exclusively, to live with him *almost as if* they were married. Almost isn't the same thing, she thought.

"What?"

She snapped her head up to meet his eyes and realized she must have spoken out loud. "I have to think about all this," she told him. "I didn't realize it would be so difficult to choose between now and the future."

"I know," he agreed then kissed her softly on the lips. "I know, *cara.*"

Under the golden Italian sun, Maria blossomed along with the olive trees. Her days were long and sun-filled and productive, but at the same time so much more tranquil than they'd ever been in Washington.

She wore loose canvas pants rolled up at the ankles, a white cotton shirt that fell comfortably over her hips, sandals and let her hair fall free, blown dry by the wind after shampooing. She'd never felt as perfectly free in her life.

It seemed strange that by risking all she'd ever imagined for herself she felt more alive than ever.

Risky.

That was the word she pulled out of the air to describe her situation. She accepted it. Although whether or not she was with Antonio, she longed for his touch with feverish intensity, longed to let him take her and make love to her without restraint—she wasn't foolish enough to believe she could have a real future with him.

One special man. One romance upon which to build a lifetime of trust and companionship. That was what she'd wanted for herself. One man who would make her his wife and give her children to love and nurture.

If she gave all of herself—body, heart and soul—to *Il Principe,* she might still marry someone else, someday. But it wouldn't be the same.

Her husband might well accept that there had been another man in her life. But she would know.

It wouldn't be right. Would never be right. She would honor her marital vows when the time came. In body and spirit she would be faithful to her husband. But the memory of Antonio would haunt any other relationship she might ever have. It would be his eyes she'd see when she made love, his mouth kissing her, his hands roaming her body.

Never could she forget the things they'd done together. Above all, it was this knowledge that troubled her deeply.

"Signorina Maria!" a shout came from behind her.

She spun around to see Genevra's maid, Angela, running after her through the tall grass bordering the grove. *"Mi aspetti, per favore!"*

She stopped and turned to meet the obviously upset young woman. "What's wrong, Angela?"

"La Signora," Angela gasped out, switching to English, "she is in very much discomfort."

Two weeks had passed since Genevra's last migraine. During that time, she'd gone to great lengths to avoid Maria.

"Does she want me to watch Michael for her?" Maria asked.

The maid looked uncertain. "She would keep him with her if she could. But he is wanting to run and play loudly. He is just a little boy," she added, apologetically.

"She can't rest with him there, and you have work to do. I understand."

Maria also understood that Genevra didn't want her spending time with her grandson.

She had tried to ignore the woman's sharp tongue and darting looks when their paths infrequently crossed in the courtyard or the main house. Nothing Maria had been able to do pleased her. But that didn't change the fact that Antonio's son needed proper care.

"I'll take Michael and see if we can find his father. Tell your mistress that you're taking him to Antonio. She might not object then."

Angela smiled, looking relieved. "*Si, grazie. Grazie mille,* Signorina Maria."

"I'll be along in a moment. There are a few things I need to do first."

As Angela ran back through the groves, Maria finished noting her most recent thoughts for the Boniface campaign on the palm-sized electronic notebook she always carried with her. Ten minutes later, she clicked the tiny computer closed, slipped it into the hip pocket of her pants and turned back toward the main house.

Striding along the pavement, she thought more about the Boniface American launch. Half her mind focused on possible strategies, appealing themes, trendy hooks. The other remained on the road, bordered on either side by low stone walls that wound like drunken serpents across the hilly landscape.

Something to do with the terrain, she mused. Something to do with tradition. Like this road that had stood the test of time and still carried people from village to village, and finally to the sea and from there to Greece, Egypt, the world beyond. Something to do with family and the love and tradition of fine food.

But nothing jelled in her mind. Not yet. With a shrug she let it go just as a sleek, road-hugging black car was weaving down the hillside between the walls toward her. The Ferrari slowed as it neared her.

"*Ciao!*" Antonio called out the open window as he pulled up alongside her. "Heading back to the house now?"

"Angela caught up with me a few minutes ago. Your mother is having another bad spell."

Antonio's dark brows rose. "She sent Angela to fetch you? That's a good sign, no?"

"Not exactly. I think the women of the household took it upon themselves to send for me. Angela's telling your mother that they're bringing Michael to you."

He frowned. "She'll be furious when she finds out they've lied to her."

Maria leaned the heels of her hands against the side of the car and stretched out her calves. "They're not lying. I'm bringing your son to you...eventually. You need to spend more time with him anyway," she stated firmly.

Antonio stared at her in astonishment. "You're *ordering* me to spend time with my son?"

"No. I'm suggesting. I know you are busy, Antonio, but if I keep him with me for a couple of hours while you take care of business, then you can have lunch with him. By that time your mother should be feeling better."

"All right," he agreed, an amused smile teasing up the corners of his full lips. "Perhaps I should make a habit of *doing lunch* with my son."

"You'll both enjoy it," she predicted.

"*Via!* Get in. I'll drive you the rest of the way back to the house."

Maria ran around the car and slipped down into the body-hugging passenger seat. The door closed with a solid, resonant clack. She marveled that this finely tuned machine and her own third-hand compact back home could possibly share the same name: automobile.

Even as he drove, foot pressed to the accelerator, Antonio kept up a running dialogue, suggesting a handful of ideas for introducing his product to America.

"They're all good," she remarked, nibbling the nail of her unoccupied hand, "but not quite right."

"What do you mean?"

"If there wasn't so much competition, I'd immediately try for an endorsement by a famous chef. Then we'd just concentrate on getting the oil in use, starting with highly visible American restaurants. There are several popular chains we might try first.''

"That could work, don't you think?'' he asked, taking the last corner before the estate's gate.

"Not really. The market studies I've requested are already indicating that home cooks—your main target—already have their favorite brands. And they're pretty loyal. Unless you can offer them something unique, something to make it worth their experimenting with a new product, you won't win them over to yours.''

He frowned, his eyes darkening dangerously. At first she thought he was angry with her for shooting down his concept, then she realized that his gaze was focused through the windshield, beyond the property's gate.

She lifted a hand to shade her eyes from the sun blazing through the glass, caught a glimpse of dark green, then a cap identical to every other man's in the village. But she immediately thought of only one person.

"You don't suppose—''

"I couldn't tell who it was,'' Antonio interrupted. "But there was definitely a man standing just off the side of the road. He stepped behind a tree when he saw us coming.''

"It could have been Marco.''

"Or a hundred other men,'' he ground out, but looked worried nonetheless.

"You don't think he's violent, do you?'' she asked, scanning the brush, seeing nothing.

"No. But I don't know why he or anyone else would be standing out here, half a mile from town. Buses don't stop to pick up passengers along this stretch of the road, and there are no other houses until you hit the edge of Carovigno.''

"And if someone was innocently walking by, why would he hide?'' she thought out loud.

"Exactly.'' Antonio's blue eyes crackled with anger.

"I'm going to have a look around. Stay in the car. Keep the doors locked." He brought the car to a screeching stop, swung open the driver's door. "Keys." He pointed to them in the ignition as he smoothly bolted up from the seat. "Take off if there's trouble. Call the *carabinieri* from the house."

Maria's heart leapt at the urgency in his tone. She clenched her hands in her lap as she watched Antonio race around the front of the car then disappear behind a tall hedge.

She looked around. Listened. Saw or heard nothing. Counted to ten...then to ten again. Still nothing.

Finally, Antonio reappeared a hundred yards down the road. He jogged back to the car.

She leaned across the driver's seat to unlock the door for him. "Well?"

He climbed in with an exasperated growl. "No sign of anyone. I'm almost certain it was Marco, though. Right height, coloring, posture." He swore in Italian. "My men have some explaining to do."

Maria blinked, sensing he was right. If it had been someone innocently wandering by, why would he have hidden? She feared sinister intentions without knowing why. A shiver wracked her body, although the sun was warm and bright overhead.

As soon as they reached the house, Antonio pulled the Ferrari to a dust-swirling stop and ran for the main house. Maria followed breathlessly.

"I'll go and get Michael," she called to Antonio as he disappeared into his office.

She heard him speaking almost immediately to his assistant. "Get Gino and Lucio on their cell phone."

Maria continued on through the house to the kitchen where she found Angela making tea for her mistress.

Michael was sitting in his high chair, munching on a

biscuit. "'ria, 'ria!" he squealed delightedly at the sight of her.

"Hello, handsome," she returned the greeting. "Having a snack, are you?"

He presented a soggy fistful of crumbs to her. *"Mangi…mangi…mangi!"*

"No thank you. Don't want to spoil my lunch," she responded cheerfully then turned to Angela. "I'll take him now. Antonio is in his office, but it looks as if he'll be pretty busy for a while."

She hesitated, wondering if now was an opportune time to fish for some much-needed information. "I rarely see Genevra in the main house or the courtyard. Am I wrong in assuming she's avoiding me?"

Angela's timid gaze shifted away from her. She poured boiling water over tea leaves. "La Signora, she spend more time in the little villa these days. I think she very busy," the maid answered diplomatically.

"Busy doing what?"

Angela tipped her head from side to side indecisively. "It's just she worry a lot. And she sad, of course."

"About what?" Although Maria was sure she knew.

"She miss Signora Anna. They very close. Like real mother and daughter. I think she would like another wife for her son, and to give her more grandbabies."

"But what does that have to do with me?"

"You are very nice, I think, but not a princess, Signorina Maria." Her tone was both diplomatic and an apology.

Maria frowned, confused. "I'm not a *princess?*"

"That is what La Signora say. Anna, she too was from the…" She stumbled over the word. "…aristo—?"

"Aristocracy," Maria supplied.

"Si. She was all that before she married young Antonio. She was beautiful and kind and very good to La Signora. But now, her son brings another woman into their home.

And she is an American, a working woman and…'' Angela sighed.

Maria accepted one of Michael's less-soggy cookies and bit into the dry end. "And not a princess."

What was she to do to win this woman over? Buy herself a title? Ridiculous.

Maybe she should just stop trying to please her. After all, in the long run did it matter whether or not Antonio's mother resented her presence here? She had only obligated herself to six months. She might even find a way to shorten the time, if she finished her work here sooner. Once her job was done, she'd be free to leave Italy and she needn't please anyone but herself.

And wasn't that the most sensible way to run one's life?

"Do not feel badly," Angela said with a comforting touch on the arm. "In La Signora's eyes, no one can replace *La Principessa*."

Maria sat heavily on a kitchen chair as Angela rushed from the room with her mistress's tray. "Well, that was reassuring," she muttered.

Eight

Antonio paced the gleaming, gray-flecked marble floor of his office. He was furious, ready for battle.

At a knock on his door, two men walked in, caps humbly clutched in grimy hands. As was common in the region, his field hands carried shotguns strapped over their shoulders as they rode noisy Vespas along the back roads. As handy for picking off a few pigeons for dinner as to use for defense of property. The wolves that, at one time, had ravished sheep and goat herds, had been hunted all but to extinction. Only the two-legged variety remained.

"So, how did it happen?" Antonio demanded, speaking in their southern dialect.

Lucio, the senior of the two stepped forward like a soldier facing his general. "We were outside the house in Carovigno. One of the Serilos, Frederico I am sure, came out. I followed him. Gino stayed behind to watch Marco. We didn't realize he'd given us the slip until you called."

Then it was him, most probably, Antonio thought. "Have-you seen Marco doing anything that might give us a clue what he's up to?''

"Maybe nothing." Gino shrugged. "They go to *mercato,* to their family's shop down the road, or home. Sometimes to a bar. Nothing mysterious in that."

"No," Antonio agreed. "Nowhere else?"

"To the beach twice, the two of them. They prance along the sand in their Speedos, talk to the pretty girls. Sometimes, go off for a while with one. *Non importa.* The usual." Gino's eyes sparkled with shared male satisfaction.

So the Serilos had gotten lucky romantically, Antonio thought. What harm was there in that? It didn't even hint at sinister intent.

But something told him to remain watchful.

"So, what do we do?" Lucio asked.

"Keep an eye on them a while longer. I want to know why Marco took the trouble to walk a half mile out of town and stand outside my house without talking to anyone."

A man with a mind to do mischief might create trouble in the groves. Destroy a portion of the crop. Poison trees or soil. Who knew what the *idiota* had in mind.

He'd tell his field managers to be vigilant.

"There you two are!"

Maria looked up to see Antonio approaching through the garden.

She'd brought Michael outside to play near the fountain. They'd folded sheets of printer paper from her office to make little paper boats. Michael had delighted in sailing his miniature armada across the glistening blue pool, splashing waves to make them go faster. He'd thoroughly soaked himself, but the sun was warm and she knew he'd dry out in minutes.

"We're sailing the high seas," she explained.

"I see you are. Looks like a few of your vessels have sunk, Michael."

The little boy splashed all the more energetically to demonstrate the game to his father. Another ship scuttled.

Maria lowered her voice. "Did you find out anything?"

"Not much. My watchdogs did lose Marco, so it's possible that was him we saw at the gate. Why he'd be lurking around I have no idea."

"Would he go so far as to break into the house?"

"Possibly. He stole before, why not again? My father's coin collection is worth a great deal," he thought out loud. "Then there are the paintings my grandfather collected over the years, hanging throughout the main house. Any one of them could bring six figures at auction, five on the black market. It's possible he is watching the *masseria* to find the best time to make his entrance."

"Who is watching us?" a sleep-thickened voice asked in Italian.

Maria spun around. Genevra Boniface stood in the path to the rose garden.

"You're feeling better, I hope," Maria said.

The woman ignored her. "Tonio, what is this watching and sneaking business about?"

"Nothing that should worry you, Mama. Marco Serilo has been seen around the property, we think. He caused Maria some concern the other day at market. We're just keeping an eye on him."

One heavy black eyebrow shot up. The woman turned to Maria. "He caused you concern. How is that?"

Maria sighed, sensing that no matter what she said, La Signora would find fault with it. "He was asking a lot of personal questions about the family."

"Of course he asks after the family," she snapped. "He used to work for us. Marco is a good boy. He only wants to know that we're all well."

Although she'd been prepared for the rebuttal, it still stung. "I didn't mean to accuse him without justification. It just seemed odd, the types of questions."

"Did he ask if I was well?" Genevra asked, switching without noticeable difficulty to English.

"Yes, he did. But he also wanted—"

The woman interrupted by throwing up her hands in a gesture of dismissal. "You see. He is a sweet, concerned boy. He got himself into trouble before. Boys do that. But he would like to be forgiven and come back to work for us. We could hire him to serve at the party, no?" She looked to her son for agreement.

"Mama, Marco is charming I'll grant you. But he's not honest, not to be trusted as a member of this household. He stole from us and from our staff. And he used my name for his own gain."

"If Anna were here, she would stand up for him."

Antonio's face went as white as the marble bench on which Maria sat.

She held her breath, too shocked by the woman's insensitivity to say anything at first. At last, she tried to find healing words for Antonio's sake.

She turned to Genevra. "I'm sure your daughter-in-law was a very forgiving person, but—"

"More than that," Genevra retorted. "Anna, she was the perfect wife. The perfect daughter. *E bella, bella!* So beautiful. She gave me the handsomest grandson." She stroked Michael's head lovingly as he ran past her, a soggy boat in paw.

Maria swallowed. The implication was clear enough.

Anna had been faultless; Maria was not. She would never live up to the memory of the departed princess, who could do no wrong. She felt the solid, reassuring weight of Antonio's hand on her shoulder.

"Mama," he said evenly, "we all loved Anna. But I don't think, as good a person as she was, even she would have overlooked Marco's indiscretions."

"Perhaps," Genevra allowed, then turned back to Maria. "I will take Michael with me now. Look at him, wet and cold, poor child. You should have taken care to keep him out of the water. His mother would never have neglected him so.''

''Mama!''

But she had already wrapped the little boy in the towel Maria had ready beside the fountain. The child screeched for his paper boats, but his grandmother energetically carried him off, chattering at him in Italian. Something about dirty toys and children dying of pneumonia from getting wet.

What a terrible woman, Maria thought to herself. But of course she couldn't criticize Genevra in front of her son. ''He was having such fun,'' was all she could say.

Antonio put his arm around her. ''Yes, he was. I'm sorry she was so harsh with you. Anna could do no wrong in her eyes.''

''Obviously.''

''I'll speak with her about being less critical, especially with regard to Michael. If I'd let him sail boats in the fountain, she might have scolded me, but with a laugh.''

Maria sighed. ''She clearly feels threatened by me, although she shouldn't.''

''Because, even if you tried, you couldn't take me and Michael away from her?'' There was a daring twinkle in his eyes.

She accepted the challenge. ''If I wanted you, I could have you. And your adorable Michael would come in the bargain,'' she boasted, not sure if she really believed her own words.

''Oh?'' He laughed. ''All you'd have to do is give us one of your pretty smiles, and we'd fall victim to your feminine wiles. Is that it?''

''Something like that.'' She fluttered her eyelashes at him outrageously. Flirting was fun and easy with Antonio. And now, in the garden, in the middle of the day, it seemed safe enough.

Antonio folded his muscled arms over his chest and stood with feet planted wide, as if bracing himself for a linebacker's block. "Give me your best shot."

Maria's cheeks warmed at the suggestion. Was he actually daring her to try to seduce him? "This is silly. I can't play this game."

"Of course you can," he said, looking boyishly impish. She could see so much of Michael in him. An image of the cookie-in-fist rascal who had offered her his soggy treat. "You say you wish to find a husband and marry. Do you think that happens without some effort on the woman's part? Without her using her most sensual charms?"

"I always thought marriage was the result of a natural and gradual coming together of two personalities, rather than a concerted effort to seduce." She was beginning to worry now. Without Michael here with her, was daylight enough to protect her?

She looked around. Absolutely no one was within sight. Where were servants when you needed them? The garden was theirs alone.

She wasn't afraid of Antonio. Not exactly. But being alone with him summoned up all sorts of treacherous feelings inside of her. And when he smiled at her, when that mellow, taunting tone in his voice came at her, all she could think of was that night when he'd brought her champagne and a lovely negligee. And he'd shown her how exciting making love could be.

Someday, she reminded herself.

Not now.

Please…not with a man who isn't ready to share his life.

She looked up out of her troubling thoughts at Antonio. He seemed to be standing just as still as a moment before, but several paces closer. How had he done that? She frowned.

"What's the matter, Maria? Not up to the challenge? What are you afraid of? We're out in the middle of a garden. Any of my groundskeepers might come along any moment. You don't think I'd risk being caught with my pants down, do you?''

She looked around again, running the tip of her tongue between suddenly parched lips.

Even though the garden seemed secluded, with hedges and rose bushes providing some measure of privacy, the house was still visible from where they stood. So was much of the rest of the property including the clusters of smaller villas, sheds and courtyards within the high stone walls. If she could see these places, anyone standing there might be able to see them.

''All right,'' she said cautiously. ''How do I know when I've won?''

''Ah!'' He grinned, delighted that she'd taken up his gauntlet. ''Let's see now. You win if I should either be reduced to begging or—'' He raised a finger to cut off her objections. ''Or, if you should detect clear physical response to your seductive ways.'' His glance dropped suggestively.

She shook her head, laughing. ''This is going to be easy.''

Antonio stood at attention, looking absolutely serious. ''I'm in complete control.''

As he'd pointed out, what harm was there when they were in such a safe location?

''All right,'' she said, strolling around him, hands clasped behind her back. She studied him from his full dark head of hair to his nicely muscled biceps, tight butt and tanned feet in espadrilles. Quite an impressive male package, no argument there.

Maria stopped dead in front of him, stood as tall and straight as he. Slowly, she let a smile lift her lips, saw a responding tremor of his lips. But he cleared his throat and rearranged his mouth into a straight, uncompromising line.

''Almost,'' she cooed. ''What about this?'' She took his

hands in hers and brought them to her hips then linked her fingers up and behind his neck and swayed suggestively. "We could dance."

"No music." His voice was a trifle husky.

"I'll hum." She did, and she could almost feel his palms begin to sweat.

"You're not playing fair," he accused, lifting his hands a safe distance from her undulating midsection.

"All's fair in love and seduction," she teased.

"I suppose, but…Maria, maybe we shouldn't…um… I didn't expect you to—" He was following her hand as she brought it to her throat and started to unbutton the top two buttons of her blouse.

She had no intention of going any further than revealing the little swell of skin just above the curve of her lace bra. Compared to what women wore at the beach, it was nothing.

"Ah, *dio!*" Antonio moaned, apparently not thinking of beaches and bikinis.

She smiled, rather pleased with her effect on him. Maybe she wasn't through with him yet.

Maria reached up behind his neck and pulled him down on the bench with her—below the line of shrubbery. Before he could react, she moved in so close that their lips were nearly touching. She blew a puff of air across his lips, teased a corner of his mouth with the tip of her tongue.

He groaned, swore…and fell on her, his kisses ravenous.

But she was ready for him.

Immediately, she brushed her hand down the front of his zipper, pressed it over the rigid shape beneath. "I'd say, *that* is evidence enough," she whispered between his lips. "*I win!*"

Antonio's eyes widened, darkened, pierced through her as she started to draw away from him. "You're not going to just leave me like this!"

"As you said, Principe, this is far too public a place to be caught with your pants down."

For the first time in her life, she felt the absolute, awesome, butt-kicking power of a woman over a man. What a discovery! She loved it!

Then his eyes flashed with that demonic, I'm-going-to-eat-you-up look.

She leapt away from him. "No, Antonio. It was a game, remember. And I have come to do a job."

He didn't move for a moment, then nodded, backed off two steps, turned and started to walk away. "Then I'd best find myself a long, cold shower."

Giggling, Maria ran to catch up with him. "I'm sorry. That was cruel of me. But you set yourself up so perfectly. And I've never acted the tramp before. It was fun."

"Fun?" He rolled his eyes, kept on walking. Stiffly.

Time to change the subject, she thought. "What party was your mother talking about?" she asked, forced to skip on every third step to keep up with Antonio's long strides.

"I don't know," he grunted. "She mentioned something about hosting a reception for you when you arrived in Carovigno. To welcome you and introduce you to our friends in the area."

"I can't imagine she'd want to do that for me now."

"No," he said. "It does seem a little odd, given her attitude lately. But once committed to something, she rarely alters course. Maybe she feels it's the right thing to do, even if she doesn't totally approve of your being here."

"Maybe," Maria agreed, still somewhat skeptical. She supposed she'd find out soon enough.

In the meantime, there was too much work to be done to waste time worrying about the woman's motives for throwing a party in her own home, if that's what she chose to do.

Nine

As a boy, Antonio had never considered running away from home. Everything he'd ever wanted was right here in Carovigno and the surrounding Apulian countryside.

But now...with his mother plotting against the woman he'd hired to help him move his company into the twenty-first century, with his heart and body at war over that very same woman, he could wish for nothing better than to escape to a place far, far away.

He stayed away from Maria as best he could. His body simply refused to listen to his brain when he was around her. He ached to touch her, even if she seemed to be paying no attention to him. He longed to stretch out on top of her, to feel himself slip silkily inside of her. No matter the time of day or night, he dwelt on her, missed her touch, her laughter.

He remembered as if only seconds had passed, the shine in her eyes when his hands wandered to forbidden places on her body.

He knew now what obsession meant.

It was several weeks later when he walked distractedly into the kitchen and found her there alone. He came up short, gritted his teeth, then put on a cheery smile for her benefit.

"*Ciao!* The *caffè* smells good."

"Oh, hello," she said, slipping her electronic notepad into her jeans pocket. "Yes, it does. Sophia only makes it in the morning, but over the years I've gotten used to keeping a cup on my desk all day long as I work. Afternoons, I've been making my own. Would you like some?"

"*Si.*"

She had just poured a fresh, steaming cup of fragrant, dark brew for each of them when Michael toddled into the kitchen, full speed. "Hello there," she said.

"'ria!" he cried joyfully and wrapped his chubby arms around her knees, ignoring his father.

Antonio frowned. "I'm hurt. He doesn't even know I exist when you're around."

"You had him pegged from the start. He's just a flirt," she said, laughing as she picked up the little boy. She hugged him to her, and he sat back and enjoyed the lovely picture the two of them made.

"Where is your *nonna?*" Antonio asked.

"*Nonna!*" Michael pointed in the direction he'd come.

A second later, Genevra appeared in the doorway, her face chalk-white, her eyes glazed over with pain. If he had sometimes wondered how much of a plea for attention the migraines might be, he didn't doubt their authenticity now.

"Is there anything I can do?" Maria asked, looking genuinely concerned.

"I'm—I don't know. Michael has been so active all morning, and I can't get him to lie down for his nap."

"I can take him for you, if you like," Maria offered.

Genevra glanced at her son. "Tonio says you have work to do and I shouldn't interfere."

"Mama, I told you I could hire a nurse for the child. You shouldn't have to be responsible for him when you aren't feeling well."

"I don't want my grandson raised by servants!" she snapped, which cost her. She immediately squeezed her eyes shut and, trembling, sat down in the nearest chair.

"The work can wait," Maria assured her. "I can do most of what I'd planned for today this evening, after Michael's asleep. And he won't disturb me during the few business calls I need to make this afternoon."

Genevra pressed the heel of one hand to her temple, but couldn't seem to manage a response.

"Have you taken your medication yet?" Antonio asked.

"No, I was afraid it would put me to sleep."

Antonio shook his head. "I'd take Michael with me, but we're regearing several machines at the plant today. I don't like to have him down there when so much is happening. It's not a safe place for a child. I could cancel and reschedule—"

"No," Maria insisted, "you go along. *Andiamo*," she said gently to his mother, as she carried Michael along with her. "Let's get you to your room where you'll be more comfortable."

Antonio watched them leave through the kitchen window. Despite his mother's continued coldness toward her, Maria had continued to treat Genevra generously, respectfully. He wouldn't have put up with half as much!

He waited, still unsure he should allow Maria to fill in as nursemaid, in addition to handling the very demanding job he'd hired her for. It didn't seem fair, but he wasn't sure how to remedy the situation.

He watched her cross the courtyard again with Michael a few minutes later.

"Oh, you're still here," she said as she pushed through the door, and Michael raced in ahead of her.

"Thought I'd finish my coffee," he replied thoughtfully.

Maria set the little boy in his high chair and poured him a glass of milk. "Well, buddy, what are we going to do with ourselves today?"

Michael alternately nibbled happily on the cookie she had given him and sipped milk from his cup.

"I know," she said as she poured herself a cup of coffee. "We'll drive to the beach. *Spiaggia.* It's a beautiful day, and I'll bet you love to swim in the ocean."

"Spiaggia!" Michael echoed, joyfully, making splashing motions on the tray of his chair.

"Now that sounds like fun!" Antonio crowed.

"You're working, remember?" Maria stuck her tongue out at him. "We have the day off."

He considered this. "Actually, I'm not sure it's a good idea to go too far away from the house."

"What do you mean?"

He sighed. "The Serilo brothers have been keeping a low profile. But I'm still worried about them. Perhaps I should send a man with you."

"A bodyguard?" She looked surprised, doubtful.

"Just to be safe," he assured her. "Give me a moment." He strode quickly from the room, took account of the locations of all his men, then returned to the kitchen.

"New plan," he said. "Everyone is busy, and I don't want to pull men from the field. The work is too critical this time of year. I'll go with you to the beach."

"Are you sure?" she asked, nevertheless looking pleased.

"My field managers are more than capable. And I can reschedule the job at the plant for tomorrow." He smiled at her. "Besides I could use a day off. And you're always badgering me to spend more time with Michael."

"True." Her eyes slid away from his, as if upset by something.

"What's wrong? Don't you want me to come?"

She recovered instantly, shook her head and smiled. "Of course we do. It will be fun."

Maria knew how very hard Antonio worked. He deserved a break, and it was true what she'd said. It would be fun to have him along. Just the three of them.

Just like a family. Almost.

That was what had crossed her mind in the kitchen. The comparison was too easy to make, and too heartbreaking to consider for long. She ruthlessly shoved it from her mind.

They drove east toward the shore, then along the coast a short ways until Antonio found the beach he was looking for. It was located near a tiny fishing village called Specchiola—pale pink, green and blue villas of only a few rooms each and narrow, unpaved streets.

The beach here was wide and blindingly white. Wooden fishing dories basked on the sand in the hot sun, faded green and red paint peeling from their bottoms, looking like colorful beached whales. The chalky, oval skeletons of cuttlefish littered the sand, slowly breaking down and being absorbed into the grains, bleaching them whiter still.

Although it seemed the perfect spot for a picnic or swim, the place was nearly deserted. Only a few young men and women frolicked in the edge of the water further along the beach.

"When I was a boy, I used to play here with my friends all the time." Antonio gazed up at the cliffs above them, gray and rough, decorated with scrub pine and wind-torn vines. "Do you see those dark patches up there?"

Maria held a hand over her eyes to shield them from the sun. It was so bright she could hardly see the darker shadows among the crags.

"Caves?" she guessed.

"Si." Antonio dashed off to stop his son from plummeting headlong into the water. Lifting the little boy, squealing, above his head, he returned to the blanket Maria had spread out on the sand. "My mother used to be terrified. We'd explore the caves, be gone for hours. Get totally lost. Come out in different places than where we went in."

"What's in there?"

"Mostly a lot of junk now. Legend has it, pirates used to hole up in them. Hide their loot. But we never saw any."

"Still, it's exciting," she said.

"For young boys, certainly. Most of these have been abandoned for centuries. There's not much of interest in them now."

Michael was not to be deterred from his quest to reach the ocean, so Maria took him into the water, and Antonio stripped off his shirt and followed. They took turns holding him and letting him kick his little feet. Whoever was left with free hands splashed the others mercilessly.

At last the little boy was exhausted. Maria laid him on the blanket after drying him off, while Antonio planted a big canvas umbrella to shade him. She stroked his little shoulders and back, humming softly to him. Soon Michael dozed off.

Maria moved to the other edge of the blanket and closed her eyes, relishing the sun's heat on her salt-encrusted limbs. Delicious, she thought as she dozed off.

Antonio had watched as Maria so naturally mothered his little son. Suddenly it was difficult to remember a time before this moment. A time before Maria was with them, was part of the little circle of inhabitants at the masseria.

How easily she seemed to know and understand what the child needed. When the little boy had started to fuss a few minutes earlier, he thought Michael was hurt. But she instinctively understood he needed sleep.

Antonio barely dared to breathe. Such a beautiful picture, he thought, staring down at them. At *her*. A unique and exciting woman with so much tenderness to lavish on two lonely, lost males.

He knelt down beside her, touched her shoulder. She opened her eyes and gazed up at him.

"He's a beautiful baby," she murmured. "And good too."

"Michael certainly seems to like you." He couldn't imagine anybody not liking Maria. Although his mother was doing a fine job of pursuing that goal.

Why was he still hesitant to let himself feel anything lasting for this good woman? It wasn't that he believed he was cheating on Anna. His time of mourning had passed, even before he'd met Maria.

Yet it had taken her arrival in his life to banish the paralyzing numbness that had tormented him during these two years since the accident.

She'd made a difference. Somehow. She'd broken through.

And now he wanted to savor life. He wanted to feel *everything!*

But mostly what he yearned to feel was Maria. Every part of her. The intensity of his appetite amazed him. He couldn't remember feeling this urgency, this maddening need to possess a single woman. Particularly one who was so very wrong for his needs.

Perhaps it was because he'd been celibate for two years. Or maybe it was because, as he'd been teaching Maria, he'd been arousing, seducing himself.

There was more to it, though.

For it was through her that he had begun to view life differently. He now could see into the future. It was no longer just the olives that kept him going. It was no longer just the fact that he had a son who needed a father. A father who was no longer just living in the most elemental sense—breathing, eating and occasionally forcing himself to accept a few restless hours of sleep.

Michael needed a father who functioned in every way. A man who could love not just the little boy, but could teach his son what it meant to grow into a man capable of loving a woman and starting a family of his own.

Antonio's hand moved from Maria's shoulder down to her waist. She didn't tighten or move away from him as she lay on her side, facing him on the blanket. Her cool gray eyes never left his.

He looked down the length of the beach, then up the other way. The bathers had left. No one was in sight.

Slowly, he leaned over her and kissed her smooth, sun-warmed forehead. Her cheek. The rim of one ear. She lifted her chin, opening her throat to him. His lips traced the long, lovely flow of virgin skin.

Stretching out alongside her, Antonio pulled her close to him. He could hear her heart beating, feel its gentle rhythm against his chest. There was so much he wanted to say to her. But, as hard as he tried, he couldn't find the words for feelings he hadn't yet been able to translate for himself. He felt so full of her, and of himself. And so utterly confused.

He touched her again, and his fingertips tingled with heat. His lips settled over hers, and his insides turned liquid.

What is right? he asked himself. What is wrong? He couldn't sort it all out at the moment. Stop touching her. Keep on touching her. But before he could figure out what to do, she lifted her arms, wrapped them around his neck, kissed him full on the mouth.

"Maria," he breathed.

"It's all right," she whispered. Framing his face between her little palms, she sprinkled kisses across his cheeks, beneath his eyes.

Erasing invisible tears, he thought. Tears he no longer wished to shed. Tears he refused to shed. For once, all he felt was joy. Pure, beautiful joy.

She pulled a corner of the thin blanket over them. Beneath the soft shield, her fingers moved lightly, caressing his chest. They soothed his throat where it burned with words he couldn't speak. They combed through the curls of hair across his belly, leaving a delicious little path of tingles behind them. Every muscle in his body relaxed. His hands fell naturally to her hips. They felt full, filling his palms, promising more.

His arousal was hot, intense and rapid.

But his brain was thankfully still working, and it shouted loud and clear that they couldn't make love now... here...on the beach. Not when somebody could come along at any moment. Not with his son lying just feet away from them.

With a surge of regret, he tossed back the blanket, rolled away from Maria, sat up.

"What's wrong?" she gasped.

"I should go back to the villa. There's a lot of work waiting for me."

She looked at him, said nothing. And finally nodded, as if she understood it wasn't work chasing him.

"Do you think Michael would wake up if we carried him back to the car?" he asked.

Maria sat up, ran fingers through long waves of blond hair that fell nearly to her waist, and his insides clenched with desire. "He's sleeping so soundly, and it's such a beautiful day. I hate to wake him. I'll stay with him. We'll be fine. You can send a car for us in an hour."

Instead of answering her, he pulled his cell phone from the pocket of his pants, lying on the sand. He moved away a few steps, spoke into it briefly then snapped it closed.

"One of my men will be here shortly. I'll wait until then."

She blinked up at the sky, bravely, he thought. *She knows.* He was using work as an excuse to leave her. And he kicked himself for bringing her to the edge of tears.

But it was either leave or break his promise to her. He was only a man, and there was just so much self-restraint doled out to every male on the planet. Lately, he'd begun to think he'd been shortchanged.

Antonio climbed the steps cut into the cliff behind the beach, stood watching her from above. At last his man came. He left without putting himself through the agony of looking down at her again. But in his mind's eye he could picture her, stretched out on the blanket beside his son, glowing beneath the potent Mediterranean sun.

Never had Maria single-handedly designed, organized, and carried out a full campaign. She deliberated every detail, mulled over decisions endlessly. But as the time for the filming approached, she felt more and more confident that she had the project, with the staff she needed, under control.

Even so, she rarely slept much at night.

Sometimes she heard Michael crying softly to himself from the little house across the garden. Usually, he stopped almost immediately, and she would know that Genevra had picked him up, was comforting him. Other nights, when she knew the child's grandmother had taken her medication, Maria went to Michael herself. She picked up the little boy, cooing to him, knocked on Genevra's door to let her know that she had him, and brought the child back to her room. He nestled into her shoulder and eventually fell asleep as she rocked him.

One such night, Antonio's bedroom door opened as she passed by it. Their eyes met, and something in his dark, brooding gaze melted at the sight of his son in her arms. He took a step forward. She waited, barely daring to breathe for the intensity of the passion she saw in his eyes. But he said nothing, came no closer.

"Do you want to take him?" she asked at last.

He hesitated. "You're much better with him."

A tiny flame of bitterness flared up within her. "He's your child, Antonio. I won't be here to comfort him forever."

He winced as if she had struck him, but she didn't care. She had learned to face the truth, it was time he did too!

Without another word he took the little boy from her, turned and disappeared back into his room. Maria closed her eyes and wished for strength.

His manner was cool to her at first, then he'd decided that she played on the shadow at the end of the and it was never came in. Into our other when he had her and both the mode of sex to appreciate the touch of room. Michael and she was pregnant, and for the child.

Ten

After the night when he'd come upon Maria and his son in the hallway, Antonio had decided that something must change. He started making time in every day for Michael, even if it was just an hour to share breakfast with the child. He found he often ate little, he was so amused with his son's personality. They played at the table, then took a walk, just the two of them, and Antonio felt he'd never been happier.

He also stopped avoiding Maria. It had been useless, trying to put her out of his mind. When he'd stayed away from her, he was distracted with thoughts of her and got little real work done. He might as well enjoy her company while he could. The weeks were flying past. Her time in Italy growing shorter and shorter.

Thankfully, his mother's attitude toward Maria seemed to mellow, and that made life pleasanter. Genevra announced that the party she'd hinted at earlier was to be a grand reception in Maria's honor. Perhaps too late for a welcome party, but at least a show of Boniface hospitality and gratitude for Maria's help with Michael.

"I was afraid you didn't like Maria," Antonio said to her when his mother told him of her plans and the date she'd chosen.

"She is not a bad woman," Genevra admitted over her morning espresso while Antonio bounced his son on his knee. "She is good to watch little Michael when I am not able. But she is not our kind, Tonio."

He frowned. "What do you mean by that?"

She shrugged. "An American and career woman. What can I say?"

He refused to take her seriously and laughed. "Mama, you sound like such a snob. Times have changed, you know."

"In some eyes, *si*. But we must protect the bloodline. Bonifaces have spawned kings, an emperor, men and women of great power and importance in history. You must never forget this, Tonio."

He smiled good-naturedly. "I won't, Mama. Promise. At any rate, I'm glad you've finally accepted Maria's presence here. She's been working hard on my campaign, and she deserves our respect for that."

"I will give her as much respect as she deserves," she stated vaguely.

Antonio searched her expression for any sign of duplicity. But she looked away from him across the courtyard. He sighed inwardly. Perhaps he was expecting too much all at once from her. After all, she was at least making an effort, in her own way, to show Maria that she was appreciated.

The guests flowed out from the grand salon on the first floor of the main house, onto the patio and throughout the garden like many-hued flower petals scattered by the wind. Barely two weeks had passed, yet the grounds had been completely transformed. An orchestra played from beneath a green-and-white striped canopy, surrounded by blooming hibiscus and delicate orchids. Elaborate ice sculptures and tables of delicious fare had been placed at strategic locations so that guests might move about freely, sampling the delicacies and visiting without becoming crowded or having to wait in line to fill their plates.

Many locals had been hired to serve for the party, and Antonio paid all generously. Maria was touched by his munificence and by the village's respect for their prince and his family. But she still ached to feel his arms around her. Silently, she wished she could stay forever in this lovely town that seemed, in so many ways, locked within its feudal past. Here, the weather, the seasons, and the day of the week on which market fell determined so much of life.

She was dwelling on such thoughts when the orchestra first began to play in the salon and Antonio came up to her. "The first waltz, if you please?" he asked, holding out his hand for her.

Maddeningly, tears came to her eyes. A prince, a waltz, and as close to a ballroom as there existed these days. What woman wouldn't be satisfied with an evening like this?

You wish for too much, a voice whispered from her heart.

"I'd love to," she said quickly, only too late remembering she didn't know how to waltz.

But this didn't seem a deterrence for Antonio. He led her through the time-honored rhythm—glide, step, step… glide, step, step—holding her firmly yet gently, making sure she stayed within the circle of his arms as they swirled across the room amidst other couples.

He looked down at her. She tried to turn her face into his shoulder so that he wouldn't see her blinking away tears. But he brought her right hand in his up to nudge her chin with one knuckle and he looked into her eyes.

"What's wrong? Don't you like the party?"

"It's very special," she said. "I'm sorry if I'm spoiling it for you."

"You aren't." He looked suddenly angry. "Just tell me what you're thinking, Maria, that makes you so sad."

"I'm leaving."

"Eventually, I suppose." He scowled at her when she didn't respond. His features hardened. "You have a contract."

"And I will fulfill it," she assured him hastily. "But we're running ahead of schedule. The filming of your commercials will be completed within the month. By then I will have finished all the research I need to do in Carovigno, in Italy for that matter. The film editing, voice-overs, final cuts can all be done in the States. I'll complete the work in D.C. while I'm working to coordinate your print ads with the TV and radio commercials."

"I had no idea." He frowned, looking disappointed.

"Listen," she said softly, "it's for the best for other reasons too. We both know there can't be anything more between us than there's already been. We've already discussed this. I don't want you to feel you're being forced to enter into a relationship you can't comfortably commit to. And I won't give up my future for an affair—extended or otherwise. So there's no place for this relationship to go."

"I see," he said stiffly. His gaze fixed on hers, and she felt her throat constrict and tears begin to well up again. But a diplomatic cough and tap on the shoulder brought Antonio around to see who it was.

A tall, blond man stood erect, smiling. "May I cut in?" he asked in polite, lightly accented English. "That is, if the lady is agreeable."

Maria was surprised but also relieved. The interruption had come at an ideal time from her perspective. She couldn't have stayed in Antonio's arms another moment before she would have burst into frustrated sobs.

The man introduced himself as he swept Maria across

the wide expanse of parquet floor. He turned out to be a nephew of Genevra Boniface.

"Are you from around here?" Maria asked pleasantly.

"I live in Milan." He went on to tell her about teaching at the university there.

They chatted pleasantly through the next two dances, then another man tapped her current partner, and she was transferred smoothly into his arms. Again, he introduced himself formally and told her he had driven all the way from Naples expressly for the party...and to meet her. When he also informed Maria that he was single and started, as her other partner had, to describe his financial background, she became more than a little suspicious.

Maria looked across the room to where Genevra was holding court with two other young men. One turned, looked Maria's way, and gave a subtle nod of acknowledgement.

What are the odds, she wondered, *at least one of them will want a dance?*

Meanwhile, she could see Antonio standing alone on the far side of the room, scowling darkly into his drink. She wondered if he too had noticed a strange pattern.

Sure enough, after another song had finished, one of the two men who had been talking with Genevra presented himself as her new partner.

Maria smiled up at him, more curious and amused than offended by what appeared to be a well-coordinated conspiracy. "Tell me, what did Genevra Boniface say to you and your friend before you approached me?"

He looked flustered. "Ah, well, La Signora...she is most discreet. I assure you."

"Discreet about what?"

"Why...your mission. Your *causa* for coming to Carovigno." His English was stilted, but she had no trouble understanding him.

"And what cause is that?" she asked.

He seemed to lose the music's beat for a moment, but recovered quickly. "I do not wish to make the difficulty for La Signora," he whispered.

Maria's smile broadened encouragingly. "Of course not."

"She confided in me, almost exclusively, that you are interested in finding a husband." He kept his voice low. "I couldn't believe, as attractive as you are, *signorina,* and with your wealth, that you had been unable to find a mate in America."

Maria's mouth dropped open.

"But," he continued proudly, "she explained how you favor Italian men, which is quite understandable."

"I see." This smile took more effort. "And you are interested?"

He grinned, nodding energetically. *"Si!"*

"What if I told you that I wasn't wealthy? That I own no property other than secondhand furniture and a ten-year-old compact car?"

He blinked at her, looking confused. "I suppose La Signora, she could have been mistaken. Perhaps that is why she so generously offered to provide a dowry?"

"A *dowry?*" Maria choked out the words. The room turned a noxious shade of red. Then tilted and pitched beneath her feet. Maria grabbed the man's jacket lapels for support. "A dowry."

"*Si,* when you marry she is promising to give the groom fifty-thousand American dollars. Most generous, yes?"

Maria swallowed and finally managed, "Most...yes!" She looked around frantically for Genevra, but the eager matchmaker seemed to have disappeared among the guests, perhaps sensing she'd been discovered. Or maybe like a heat-seeking missile, honing in on another prospective suitor.

Meanwhile, her partner seemed unfazed by her confessed

lack of funds. "So," he purred in her ear, dragging her closer, "we can be frank, no? You like Rufio?"

Maria slipped down and out of his arms. "I like you very much, Rufio. But not enough to marry you. Excuse me." She gave him a brief, teeth-gritting smile and dashed across the room.

Before she was halfway to the other side, Antonio intercepted her. Seizing her arm, he pulled her up short. "Where are you off to so quickly, Miss Popularity?"

She glowered at him. "Let me go. I have a bone to pick with your dear mother."

"Really. Not enough men to go around? Could be you're monopolizing them all."

She couldn't believe it—he chose this moment to turn into the green-eyed monster! Men!

"Oh, yes," she snarled, "I've been enjoying myself immensely. Being auctioned off to every eligible bachelor in Italy is just what I've always wanted."

Antonio's grip weakened, and she shook herself free. But when she started past him, he stepped to one side to block her. His expression looked dangerously stormy. "Woman, what are you talking about?"

"I'm referring to your mother's real motive for throwing this little bash. Me!"

"But of course, she planned everything in your honor. She consulted me on every detail beforehand, to make sure you would approve."

"Along with the ice sculptures and lovely menu, did she happen to mention she was putting a fifty-thousand-dollar bounty on my head?"

Antonio's electric-blue eyes turned incredulous. "*Su!* What the hell are you talking about, Maria?"

"Genevra has offered money to any man who can get me to marry him. Do you suppose there's a somewhat lesser amount waiting should one of them talk me into bed for a night?"

"I don't believe it."

"I," Maria stated firmly, "believe it. I don't put anything past that woman. I'm having a word with her. Now!"

"Wait!" But it was too late. Maria was off at a run to
do battle. Gown, formal satin heels and all.

Antonio cursed under his breath, cursed again for good
measure and took off after her. He had serious doubts
whether either of the two females would survive the next
hour if he didn't interfere.

But Maria was quick.

By the time Antonio fought his way across the salon
between clusters of guests, he was horrified to discover Maria had pulled his mother away from her friends and was
speaking to her in a low tone. He grimaced, not eager to
shed his own blood in the mêlée to come.

Perhaps the situation would resolve itself? Dreamer! No,
he would step in if things got physical, although he had
trouble imagining his aristocratic mother duking it out with
little Maria.

Still...Maria looked ready for a good brawl.

He circled the two women cautiously, desperately trying
to pick up a few words without too obviously eavesdrop-
ping. His mother's expression was grim as she listened to
Maria, who spoke animatedly, her hands flying to emphasize her words. She looked very Italian. Very cute. He had
trouble not smiling.

He moved closer, stepping behind his mother to hear
better.

From here he could see Maria's expression, and he was
astonished to see that she was smiling. If she wasn't enjoying herself, she was putting on a damn good show.

He moved closer.

"I understand your concern," Maria was saying. "But
there's no reason to worry about my taking either of your
men away from you. In two months I'll have finished all I

need to do here. Then I'll return to the States. Alone. I'm here to work, for no other reason.''

Antonio searched her eyes desperately for any sign of her pleasant smile weakening, but could find none. It broke his heart. He had hoped that he might still convince her to stay with him. But she sounded so sure of herself, so set on doing what she felt was the right thing.

He didn't stand a chance.

Two months. They would be eight weeks—one hundred sixty-eight hours each—of longing and frustration. If she'd given in and slept with him, he could at least have hoped to get her out of his system. Most affairs, he knew from his own premarital experiences, and those of friends, burned themselves out in a few months.

Why was it too much to ask for just an average length affair with the woman? He felt like punching out one of those damn ice sculptures.

If he'd been less than honorable, he might have lied to Maria like other men. Told her he loved her and promised her they'd marry. Perhaps use his mother as an excuse for not announcing their engagement immediately. He might have asked her to give him time to warm Genevra up to the idea of their marriage. While she granted him those weeks, he would be enjoying all the benefits of having a fiancée—including her sweet body.

Unfortunately, he was not that kind of man.

Antonio tuned back in on the conversation between the two women while he picked up a plate and pretended to select food from the buffet.

His mother was speaking in careful English. ''I was only trying to encourage suitors for you, Maria. Any mother would do as much.''

''But you're not my mother,'' Maria pointed out gently. ''And I'm not interested in marrying any of these men.''

''You are a pretty young woman. You should have gentlemen friends. I see no one coming to call on you.''

"I'm working while I'm here in Carovigno. I don't want the distraction of dating." She laid a hand on his mother's arm. "I know how close you are to your son and grandson. Even if I had the power to take them from you, I would never do that."

He turned to see his mother's expression.

She held herself proudly erect and spoke solemnly. "Perhaps you do not intend to hurt this family. But I know what I see. You are in love with my Tonio. He has been lonely so he is drawn to you. But he will never marry again. You will see." She nodded wisely. "You will see, Maria Mc-Pherson."

Maria stood silently, watching Genevra walk away from her. Her gaze drifted to the floor. She didn't move.

Antonio walked over to her. "I'm sorry. She speaks her mind. At times it's not appropriate or even the truth."

Maria glanced up at him, her eyes rimmed with pink but dry. "I expect she's right on target this time."

Antonio shook his head. "She's right about my not wanting to marry again. But the rest—"

"You mean about my being in love with you?" Maria laughed, but he detected no humor in the clipped, unnatural sound from her throat. "I used to believe that one person couldn't possibly love another who didn't return their love. It seemed like asking for pain. How could a person have so little respect for herself? But I can see you don't love me, and…" Her beautiful silver-gray eyes filled with tears. Words trembled on her lips then dissolved. "Oh, damn you, Antonio…"

She turned and ran from him, past a glistening sculpture of a butterfly, past servers carrying trays laden with caviar and delicate pastries. He glanced at his mother and saw that she had been watching them.

Shooting her a look intended to remind her that he was his own man, Antonio ran after Maria.

Eleven

Maria's heart felt as if it had been fed through a paper shredder. Was she so utterly transparent? Did everyone who even looked at her when she was with Antonio immediately know how smitten she was?

What a dreadful mistake she'd made coming here! She'd understood from the beginning that Antonio wanted an intimate relationship. Purely physical—no promises, no obligations. He'd been honest about that much.

She knew it! Yet she'd walked boldly into his world, and now she'd made everything worse, all but admitting that she'd fallen in love with him. She had no one to blame but herself for her shattered heart. What had she been thinking?

Stopping only long enough to kick off each of her dress pumps, Maria ran barefoot across the garden and out through the estate's main gate. She kept on running up the road toward town, through narrow, deserted streets. Up and up twisting alleys of stone that smelled of bread, mold and, she realized with revulsion, urine.

Not much had changed here since the Middle Ages...certainly not in the men bred by this town. Men like Antonio who ran their lives according to their own whims or desires.

She swore under her breath, fought back tears, ran on through dark streets putting space between herself and the *masseria,* as her feet began to hurt from pounding against the hard earth and cobbled roads. At last, out of breath, she crested the hill on which Carovigno had been built millennia ago, rounded the ancient castle's walls, and started down the other side, through twisting paths and rubble.

It seemed odd that she had seen only a few shadowy figures moving through the streets in all this time. The entire town must have been invited to the party. And every eligible bachelor had undoubtedly been informed of her *availability!* She groaned at the humiliation.

At last she ran out of civilization, found herself in a steeply sloping field crowded with boulders and almond trees. Olive trees ranged below and off into the dark distance. Among them were a few little conical-roofed huts of what looked like stone blocks. Collapsing into the grass, desperately pulling air into burning lungs, she dissolved into tears. She wished she'd never had a twenty-fifth birthday. A birthday that had brought such a maddening, self-centered, amazing man into her life.

After a while, she heard ragged breathing from above her, then footfalls skidding down the rocky hillside. Her stomach clenched. Hastily, she wiped the dampness from her cheeks and tried to melt into the grass.

"You never...told me you'd...gone out for cross-country," a deep voice gasped.

"Go away, Antonio," she muttered.

"Are you upset because my mother told you what I had already confided in you?"

"I said, go away!" There wasn't a thing he could say

to make her like him again, she told herself. Not a thing. "How did you find me anyway?"

"That white dress…it stands out in the moonlight like a beacon. I've been…*Dio!*…tailing you since you hit the main road into town. Nearly killed me!" He gulped down a few more breaths, took a seat beside her on the ground before managing to continue. "Is she right?" he asked softly. "Are you in love with me, Maria?"

She twisted around in the grass and glowered at him. "I hate you!"

More to the point, she hated that he looked so damn good in a black tuxedo, in the moonlight, with chunks of granite as a backdrop. How was a girl supposed to respond rationally to a man under such circumstances?

"You hate me," he stated, studying her expression intently.

She had to look away from him. "Listen, I'm not about to feed your male ego. Let's just leave it that we're different. Rather, what we want from life is different."

"What if I told you I'm not sure what I want?" he said in a voice that drew her in.

She shook her head fiercely, fighting the feelings. "I don't believe that. At the very least, you know what you *don't* want. You don't want a wife. And you don't want more children. And those are exactly the things I do want— marriage and a family."

He opened his mouth to say something, but she barreled on.

"A conventional marriage, as in two people who love each other and work together to raise their children, and trust that the other person will be there for them when times are rough. Maybe you're still hurting from tragedy, but I don't really believe that. Not after seeing you these last few months. Maybe it's just that marriage isn't exciting enough for your royal blood. Doesn't give you enough freedom or whatever rationale you want to use." She turned to face him. "But this is my life too, Antonio, and I have a choice, dammit!"

He slid a few inches away as if to better observe her. Nothing in his eyes or the set of his mouth helped her read his thoughts. Maybe it was better for her sanity that she couldn't.

"Of course you have a choice," he said at last.

"Don't patronize me!" She pounded both fists hard into his chest in protest, shot to her feet, ready to run. But he was up too, fingers latched around her wrist before she could take a step away.

"Oh no, you don't. I'm not chasing you another mile through the countryside tonight." He spun her around to face him again, held her tightly against his chest. "We need to talk about this."

"I don't want a short-term affair with you or any other man!"

"What about a long-term affair with a man who cares deeply for you?"

She sniffled and glared up at him. She hadn't heard the words love or commitment or marriage yet. But she sighed, understanding that he was trying, in his own way, to compromise. It just wasn't enough for a lifetime.

"Listen," she whispered, "I know you believe that's the most you can give. I respect that. But what if we made love and I ended up pregnant? Conveniently, you've already stated your position—no marriage. So what would happen then, *Principe?*"

He looked incredibly sad. "I...Maria, I wouldn't expect—"

"You wouldn't what?" she interrupted, suddenly overcome by tears, furious she hadn't been able to contain them. "You wouldn't expect me to have the baby, is that it? I'd be given your royal permission to terminate my pregnancy. And wouldn't that just fit in perfectly with my plans for having a family?"

He hauled her in closer and gave her one good hard shake. "Stop it!" he shouted. "Maria, listen to me for just one minute."

She gasped for breath but the tears seemed unstoppable.

"I'm sorry for the turmoil I've caused you. But I'm grateful, more grateful than I can say for knowing you. You've given me hope. Can't you see that?"

She swallowed, then swallowed again. No. She wouldn't let him do this to her, talk her out of her fury. It felt good to shout and spit and pound on something...and, oh damn, why was he staring at her that way?

She looked away to avoid his steady blue gaze. She didn't want to feel anything for him...not sympathy, not love, certainly not passion.

"Maria, I honestly don't know what to do about us." He crushed her to his chest when she tried to pull away. "Please believe me. I've struggled with these feelings from the moment we met. If I hadn't been thinking of your well-being that first day, I would have left you in that Washington office after announcing that Marco wouldn't be making his appearance."

"You should have!" she snapped, lips pressed to his lapel.

"You're here, at least in part, for your own benefit. For your career. If we just keep our heads, you'll walk out of this job with one scorcher of a résumé, and you know it."

"If you really care what happens to me, why have you done nothing but try to seduce me ever since I came here?" she demanded.

He held her and didn't answer for a long time. Clouds scudded across the moon. A dog barked in the distance. The air shifted, swirled in warm eddies around her bare shoulders. She breathed. Waited for him to say anything at all that would make sense of this mess.

"You are a very desirable woman, *cara*. Please don' place all the blame on me. I accept full responsibility fo

my actions. But for my emotions, I cannot speak. They are
what they are.''

She hated this feeling of being slowly drawn to his side
of the battle, losing sight of her own best interests. Why
was it always the woman who looked out for everyone
else...at her own expense?

"Having an affair with me or anyone else isn't going to
cure you of grief." She reached out to touch his cheek then
pulled her hand back quickly. Such gestures, she couldn't
afford, only got her deeper in trouble. "I just woke you up.
Now you need to find someone willing to play on your
terms.''

The words burned across her lips. She hated what she
was telling him. Go find yourself another woman. But it
was the only way she could advise him. Clearly, this was
not a man for whom celibacy was a permanent choice. And
if it wasn't her in his bed, well then...

"It's not as easy as that," he stated, studying her intently. "I don't want anyone else. Other women don't affect me the way you do." He brought his hand around the
back of her neck and eased her head back.

She told herself to resist. She told herself she didn't have
to stay here, didn't have to listen any longer. Didn't have
to stand on a rock-strewn hillside in the middle of the night
and be kissed.

If that was what he was about to do.

So what was taking him so long?

"You see," he said, "when you look up at me like this,
I can almost hear you asking to be kissed. Then I can't
refuse." He bent down and brushed his lips lightly over
hers. The bare soles of her feet lost all sense of contact
with the pebbly ground. Her head seemed to float free of
her body. Balance was chancy at best. Maria reached out
to grab his arm for support.

"Don't, Antonio." As soon as she felt steady she
brought her arms between them protectively.

He kissed her again. More firmly.

"You said all I had to do was say no, and you would stop. Those are the rules. *Your* rules."

"But only if you mean it," he whispered.

"*I mean it!*"

"Your body tells me otherwise."

"My body is a freakin' traitor! Stop it."

He pulled back to observe her. Slowly, she dared to look up to meet his gaze. It was a mistake. With his body so close to her, the scent of him still in her nostrils, the warmth of his arms around her, she was full of him. No longer capable of fighting off fate. And that was what she finally decided it had been.

Fate.

It came to her as an epiphany, ripe with sudden realization, rather than from lack of rational thought. Maybe it was only at that moment, that she understood the depth of her own hunger for love.

Maria closed her eyes and let this new way of looking at things sink in deeper. Like rain trickling down into drought-parched earth. Think outside of the box—that was what her training in advertising had taught her.

What if leaving Antonio turned out to be the worst mistake of her life? What if fate meant him to be her only true love, for all of her life? Maybe if she didn't risk everything for him, she'd never be given a second chance.

How often in one lifetime could a person expect to find the perfect mate? Tragically, some women never did. And here she was closing the door on a remarkable man. A man she respected, who had been good to her. How did she know that when she next opened a door, Mr. Right would be standing there? Would ever be standing there.

She was twenty-five and, technically, still a virgin. She had waited. No one had even come close to exciting her...until Antonio came along. She wanted him with all of her soul. Desperately. With every breath she took. If she walked away from him now, would she merely be denying him pleasure, or refusing herself her one chance at happiness?

"The groves down there—" she pointed, her voice husky with emotion "—they're some of yours?"

"Yes," he answered, frowning as if he didn't understand the reason for her question.

"And those little stone huts?"

"The *trulli*. Yes, they are on my property. The path below circles back toward the *masseria*."

"Are they...occupied?" she asked, lifting her chin to meet his gaze dead-on.

A dark fire flickered in his eyes. "I keep one *trullo* for myself, for pruning and harvest seasons. I sleep in the field then, as my father and grandfather did."

"Take me there."

He looked bewildered by the possible meanings of her words.

She nodded in silent answer.

"You are certain, *cara?* I know I've bullied you. I've—"

Her fingertips rested over his lips. "Been aggravatingly persistent, yes. But not bullied." She sighed and looked across the fields toward the walled main house and its surrounding buildings. "I can't be with you up there. But here, away from everyone... Please, let's go to your *trullo* and—"

He kissed her gently to silence, took her hand and led her down the hillside to the ancient stone dwelling that was as old and proud and forever as the land itself.

To an extent, the *trulli* resembled igloos. Instead of ice, they had been made of hand-hewn stone blocks. This one's cone-shaped roof was topped with a curious ball-shaped symbol in stone. As Maria ducked inside the low doorway, she caught a whiff of wood smoke then the faint aroma of herbs and flour, baked and shared within the thick stone walls for centuries.

Memories, she thought. Memories have been made here, by loving generations. Children had been nourished, the elderly cared for. And who knew how many lovers had come here to be alone, perhaps begin a new generation.

Although the structures looked dwarfishly whimsical from a distance, she could see they served a purpose. The walls appeared to be nearly three-feet thick, strong protection against the elements and, perhaps, from the wild creatures and robbers that once roamed the land.

Gradually, her eyes adjusted to the dark. Vague objects took on form within the roughly plastered walls of the single room. A small, splintery table. Two spindle-back chairs, stained with weathering. A compact, free-standing wooden cupboard. A bed.

This last had a wood frame, hemp mesh supporting the mattress, which was covered with a coarse but clean cotton ticking. She imagined from the soft bulges and hollows that it might be filled with straw.

The rustic nature of the furnishings appealed to her. Maria felt one with the ages. Sharing something precious with women through time who had sought and found nests in which to love their men.

"It's not very elegant," Antonio spoke apologetically from behind her. He wrapped his arms around her like a comfortable shawl, and she turned within them to smile up at him.

"It's perfect," she said, leaning her cheek against the hard wall of his chest.

He kicked the door closed. Cut off from the moonlight, the room went black. She felt him lean down. His lips brushed hers, delicately, carefully. "Hold on a moment," he whispered.

She felt him move away, then he was working his way around the room, shifting things on shelves. The single sharp scrape of a struck match was followed immediately by a brilliant orange glow. Shadows flew up and across the arch of aged plaster above them.

Maria met Antonio's eyes across the room. A score of emotions shimmered in his dark gaze. Defining any one of them was impossible.

"Are you frightened?" he asked.

She shook her head.

How could she be afraid of him? The way he'd always treated her let her know that he would never hurt her, at least not physically and not intentionally. What she felt in her heart was another matter. But he'd been painfully honest with her. Perhaps that was worth more than what most men gave. He'd never tried to manipulate her.

At Klein & Klein there was a saying: "Any publicity is good publicity." It didn't matter whether or not a client was misquoted, an author got a mediocre book review or an actor's latest performance was panned. You took any mention in the press you got, then put a positive spin on it.

That's how she now felt about Antonio.

He had offered her a wonderful job, a chance to see a new and exciting part of the world, and his body. His soul and his heart, he'd made clear, were his to keep. So she would take from him what he could give. She wouldn't deprive herself of the experience he offered her. And when their time together was over, she would hold her head high, walk away from him, into another life without him. He could keep what was dear to him, and she would cherish her pride.

And, if the man she was meant to marry ever did come along? Well, if he didn't understand her having slept with another man she'd truly cared for, then maybe he didn't have the compassion she'd want in a husband.

Antonio reached out to Maria and took her in his arms. A voice within scolded him for bringing her here, despite her apparent willingness. How dare he take from her the one treasure she had hoped to share with another man! But he wrestled accusing words to the back of his mind. Later, he supposed, he would kick himself. Maybe even hate himself for what he was about to do. But now he must pay attention to Maria.

He would take her carefully. He would make sure she felt only joy in these precious moments they shared. And when their time for parting came, which he hoped would not be soon, he would protect her as best he could from heartache.

And there was more he could do for her.

"Maria," he whispered, folding her in his arms.

"Yes," she breathed against his chest.

"No promises."

"I know."

"Except for one." He tenderly kissed the soft blond curls on the crown of her head. "If you should ever need help of any kind. Ever need money, advice, names of people who can help you professionally or otherwise, come to me. I won't turn you away."

She stared up at him. "I don't want your money, Antonio."

"Just remember. Someday, you may need a benefactor. I'll do anything I can to help you, *cara*. Anything."

Her eyes, bright with silver highlights among the gray irises, slid away from his. "You don't need to buy off your guilt," she whispered. "I've made my decision for my own reasons." She sighed. "Maybe it was destiny that I'd meet you and we'd have this affair before I could move on with the rest of my life."

Affair, he thought. The word sounded crass and common, beneath her. Feelings he had shut down for so very long, ways of thinking about a woman, about Maria…they soared far above the common. Except there was this hunger. This craving for her that had colored everything between them from the moment they'd met.

How could you explain that other than as pure lust?

Antonio wanted to argue with her, to shake her and shout that she wasn't just a mistress, wasn't just half of a tawdry affair. But he could grasp no satisfactory definition for what had been happening between them in the past months. A surge of frustration, of rage with himself built. But as he gazed down at her these were immediately replaced by the most basic of male needs.

He wanted her.

He needed her as he'd needed no other woman in his life.

"How do you do this to me, woman?" he growled, pressing his lips over hers with an urgency that shocked him.

He had never needed anyone. Not even Anna. Theirs had been an arranged marriage, a traditional marriage of two families, conceived by the matriarchs of the family—his grandmother and hers. Yes, he'd loved her then, and some part of him would probably always miss her. But Maria had touched places in his heart that Anna had never reached. Her power over him was frightening. And exciting.

He kissed her violently, clasped her to him with a strength that denied all his pleas that they would have no future. She didn't resist him. Returned his kisses with a heat of her own.

He felt around behind her, found the zipper of her gown, dealt with it. Raking the garment from her shoulders he sent the straps of her bra after it. Bare shouldered, lovely. The fullness of her breasts invited him. He pressed his palms over them, and she arched into them.

"You are so very beautiful."

"You don't have to say that!" she assured him, her eyes bright and eager.

"I don't have to do anything. I *want* to tell you how lovely you are, because it's the truth."

She just smiled, as if she still didn't believe him. Linking her arms up and over his shoulders, around his neck, she gazed up at him with steady gray eyes. Her breasts filled his hands, and he could feel the nipples rising, tickling the rough skin of his palms as he moved them in slow patterns over her flesh.

He wanted her as if he'd never known a woman's body before.

Lifting her from her feet, he carried her to the bed, laid her down. She let him finish undressing her, offering no resistance but letting him do all the work. He ringed her slim ankles with this fingers, smoothed them up over her calves, her knees, thighs…then back down again. Repeating the motion, he watched her eyes widen as his hands rose, caressing her long, silky limbs. Stopping just short of paradise. He could read her desire, knew she wanted more.

As did he.

There was another instant when he questioned himself. She was his employee, his guest in a country that wasn't her own. In so many ways, she was still an innocent. And she had never changed her mind about wanting a husband.

All things considered, he was her worst nightmare. He was the end of her perfect dream.

Yet even at this late moment, when his body urged him to take all she offered, when his need for her was crossing an invisible border between fiery urgency and lethal desperation, he slowed down. Gave her a chance to end it. One word from her, and he'd have escorted her back to the reception, still a virgin.

He wouldn't like it. But he would suffer without complaint. For her. One word.

She never said it.

Maria pulled him down on top of her. He was still fully clothed, and she lay beautifully naked beneath him, on his straw mattress, in the dwelling of his ancestors. Men who had fought for this land, won it from the Greeks who had originally brought the first olive trees across the Aegean to plant and nurture here. Men who had built castles to defend their countryside from Saracens, invaders from the North, and ultimately rival dukes.

From a tradition of powerful warrior aristocrats, he had been bred. They were in his blood. They were his heritage. But tonight Principe Antonio Boniface felt helpless at the touch and sight of this gentle American woman who asked so little of him. She didn't want his money, his title or property. All he could give her at this moment was her womanhood, in all its glory.

Yes, he'd shown her a great deal already because she'd been curious. Now she wanted more from him, but it wasn't curiosity that had finally placed her in his bed. She *felt* something for him. Something important and tender and maybe close to love. It was because she was so sincere, so trusting, that he didn't want to frighten her or leave her with any but the most delicious memories.

He took her slowly.

Antonio brushed his lips across hers. Kissed her throat, delicately touched his tongue to her breasts. When Maria moaned softly and rested one hand against the back of his neck as if to keep him there, he drew a swollen nipple between his lips, teased it between his teeth. She whimpered, wriggled blissfully beneath him. He moved to her other breast, teased, suckled with a hunger that left him dizzy, panting. Still she pressed his head down harder against her. He obliged.

Her hands were moving down between them. Further down. Lower still. Consciously, he followed her progress as her fingers inched beneath his belt, into his pants. He drew a sharp breath as a cool palm slid into his briefs, found him, wrapped around his erection. She moved her hand as he'd taught her, improvising now with little squeezes, heightening the intensity of his pleasure.

Antonio closed his eyes on a long, low groan, restrained himself. Intense pressure, heat in his groin paid him back. He ached, throbbed, held on for dear life.

Burying his face at her throat, he tasted her sweetly moist skin, gritted his teeth on another wave of near-release. *"Dio!"* he moaned. *"Piu lentamente! Per favore!"*

"Slower?" she asked breathlessly, stilling the motion of her hand for a moment.

"Si, it will be over too soon if you—"

She smiled sweetly as she tightened her grip a notch, her eyes sparkling as if she savored her power over him. He ached to pay her back, but other things were suddenly on his mind. Like protection.

He remembered through a steamy fog that he did have a condom in his wallet. He'd started carrying one when Maria arrived in Italy. Not, he told himself, because he intended to bed her. Sensible protection seemed more a function of his existing within the same town with her. Hell, within the same country! He'd never been able to predict what might happen when he was around her.

He rolled to one side, eased the slim leather bifold from his pocket. As she watched with interest, he took out the small foil packet and laid the wallet on the table beside the bed.

"Thank you," she said, "for thinking of that."

He nodded, too busy for conversation as he searched for the starter tear that would let him open the thing. His hands shook. He dropped the packet, picked it up off the bedding, tossed aside the foil…and only then realized he hadn't yet undressed.

"Idioto!" He felt like a fumbling schoolboy, trying out his manhood for the first time.

"I'll hold it," she said and released him to take the latex disk.

He ripped off his clothing, tossing it piece by piece onto the nearest chair. Smooth, real smooth, he chided himself, trying to pull himself together as he joined her on the bed again. She was studying the condom, running her finger around the fat rim.

"Do you want to do it?" he asked, as she seemed so intrigued.

"Don't know how," she admitted with an adorable shrug that set his heart tripping.

He showed her how to unroll it, then guided her fingers as she smoothed the whisper-thin material over him. He pretended patience. He was a mess inside.

Her eyes widened as he swelled still more. "You're so—" Maria dissolved in a fit of giggles "—large."

"Never laugh at a man's apparatus unless you follow it with that word exactly. Afraid I won't fit?" Keep it light, he told himself, though every nerve in his body was afire. If he didn't find a way to slow himself down, he'd lose control. Above all he didn't want to hurt her. Didn't want to ruin this for her.

"It's a little—" She ran the tip of her tongue over her upper lip. "—a little difficult to imagine."

"Your body will accommodate me, I promise," he said softly, brushing a wisp of hair from over her eyes. "That's the way it works. We'll fit, you'll see."

She looked more than a little skeptical but brought her hands up to experimentally smooth them across this chest. They felt warm and sent a fresh rush of heat plummeting through his gut to his loins.

He lowered himself over her but didn't yet try to enter her. With the tips of two fingers he traced the V between her delicate thighs then gently moved her legs apart. He kissed her to keep her busy while he located the delicate nubbin he'd found before and teased it until she tightened and shivered with her first climax. Now as he continued to fondle her, the flesh was saturated, blooming for him. Her fingernails bit into his shoulders as she very nearly went through the ceiling.

She was ready.

But he didn't want the next part to cause her pain. So he kissed her harder, much harder, until she was gasping and writhing beneath him. Only when she was fully occupied did he move his fingers firmly upward, quickly severing her seal. He held his hand there, pressing as against a wound. Lifting his head he searched her eyes, sparkling, eager. She showed no sign of discomfort, moved her hips tighter against his hand, as if understanding his strategy.

"The rest will be easy," he whispered. "If you still—"

She kissed him fast on the mouth. "*Per favore,* don't stop!" And she lifted her legs, linking them around his hips, opening herself to him.

More than anything in the world, what he wanted to do was plunge inside her. Dive deep and hard, leaving no doubt that he'd possessed her. If only for these few minutes.

But what she needed now wasn't that kind of lover.

He guided himself just to the opening of her womanhood. With very little pressure, he moved upward. Testing. Easing himself forward a fraction of an inch at a time. Parting her flesh as a ship cleanly, painlessly parts the waters through which it sails. Their eyes met, held, acknowledging a fusion of bodies, of souls as he continued to move upward.

He was about to ask if she was all right, when she shocked him by taking control of the situation. Locking her ankles behind his butt, she yanked him hard against her. Suddenly, he was in all the way.

Maria grinned up at him as if pleased with her participation.

There was nothing left for him to do but close his eyes and savor her hot, silky flesh folding around him. He dared not move for several minutes, for fear of immediately coming. Then he felt her begin to squirm a bit, as if uncomfortable under his weight.

He lifted himself onto his elbows and stared down at her appreciatively. "Took me by surprise."

"Good," she purred. "Is this it?"

He laughed. "No." *Dio,* he hoped not. "You're ready for more?"

"Absolutely!"

He no longer felt like talking. He had to concentrate to give her enough time to reach her peak before he did. Which would be a trick since he was already teetering on the edge like a fledgling rock climber.

From that second, he dedicated every ounce of his energy to pleasuring both of them. He lifted his hips, drawing nearly out of her then smoothly gliding inside again. He repeated the delicious motion a score of times.

Didn't stop when she gasped and heaved beneath him.

Didn't stop when she cried out his name.

Didn't stop after she'd ridden what he estimated was her fourth—fifth?—wave of shuddering ecstasy.

Only when her beautiful eyes glazed over and her fingers combed through his hair, fisting among the strands, and she whimpered with exhaustion did he plunge one final time and allow his own release.

Flames consumed him. Time lost all meaning. Dimensions exploded, breaking barriers of shape and form, so that where he was became as much a mystery as who he was, had been, or could be.

Nothing mattered but the woman lying beneath him, around him. Rapture, oneness. Heat and eternity. Sensations that made no sense, but were more real to him than anything he'd ever known.

And Maria held him through it all. Held him and didn't let him fall. And for the span of a few precious seconds he felt immortal.

Twelve

The days that followed were sun-filled, happy, richly soaked in the wine of lovemaking. The only thing that could have made Maria happier was to know that she would always have Antonio in her bed, in her life.

But she'd never been a person to view her cup as half-empty. The fact that he wanted her and no one else with him now was enough. Yes, she'd given up part of her ultimate dream for him. She was no longer a virgin. But she still believed that someday she would marry and have children of her own. Meanwhile, she could at least pretend that this exciting man was her husband. She could imagine that Michael was her son. And with this fantasy, she walked the olive groves, did her very best work and learned to be happy with each day as it came to her.

Although Genevra said nothing to Maria about her absences every evening after their last meal of the day, often served in the main house as late as nine o'clock in the traditional Italian manner, Maria realized the woman wasn't stupid. She guessed that Genevra knew Maria was meeting her son somewhere. She simply chose not to address the subject, and Maria respected the older woman's wishes by not doing so either.

Frequently, La Signora's headaches arrived during dinner, and they seemed to occur with more frequency than before. At these times, she would excuse herself from the table and ask Maria to watch over Michael, even though the child was fast asleep by that hour.

The third time this happened, Antonio set down his wineglass with emphasis. "Michael never wakes, Mama. He's fine. Have Angela look in on him once in a while. Maria has work to do."

"Work, is it?" Genevra muttered as she pushed herself up from her chair. "Think of your son, Antonio. Respect the memory of his mother!"

Maria was shocked, and could only sit and stare at the woman's retreating back. Had the warning been meant as much for her ears as for Antonio's. She turned her attention back to the table, where he sat staring at the uneaten food on his plate. Maria went to him and knelt beside his chair.

"I'm so sorry. My presence here has disturbed everything."

"No, it hasn't!" Antonio snapped. "Haven't I a right to live again? A right to happiness?" He turned eyes the color of a troubled sea down on her. "I've spoken to her about us. Reassured her. But she won't listen."

"I know," Maria whispered. "I know." Hadn't she also tried to clear the air when she'd first come to Carovigno? "Genevra obviously doesn't believe us."

"Such a childish attitude. I've explained to her that you are only here for a short time."

Tears pooled in Maria's eyes at his cruel words. Unintentionally cruel, yes, but the truth hurt no less. "She obviously doesn't believe it." She decided it was safest to change the subject. "I've been working on your print ads to follow up on the television launch. Would you like to hear what I have so far?''

He took her hand across the table. ''Yes. But in a few hours, not now.''

''Not now?'' she asked puzzled.

''This is our time. You wouldn't want to break with tradition, would you?''

She smiled. He was choosing to make love with her over talking about the work he lived for. How many women could boast a man so passionately protective of their private time?

''All right,'' she said. ''After.''

As promised, few hours later, as they lay in each other's arms in the *trullo,* free of clothing, nestled in sheets rearranged in curious patterns by their energetic play, Antonio at last said, ''Tell me about your plans.''

Maria pulled her thoughts out of a cotton-candy haze and focused on the strategies she'd been developing since she'd come to Italy. During those spring and summer months, the olives had grown to plump, shiny black globes, ripe and ready for harvesting. The fields had already begun to buzz with activity. Now it was her turn to harvest the fruit of her hard work.

''We need to go back to my office. I have something to show you.''

He groaned and tugged her closer to his muscular body, glistening with sweat from his exertions. ''You mean I have to move from this sublime position?''

''Sorry 'bout that,'' she teased, shoving him aside and rolling off the straw mattress.

They dressed and walked hand-in-hand back through the fields then the garden. It was after midnight, and no one in the household was about.

In her suite were the TV, VCR, desktop computer and graphic equipment she'd requested and used to put together her promotional package. Maria sat down at her desk. Antonio pulled up a spare chair beside her. He watched with interest as she slipped a cassette into the VCR and the TV screen lit up.

"This is the competition," she explained, as she hit the Play button on the controller.

After viewing the ads, Antonio looked worried. "So what do we do to snatch a share of the market? Are we going to be able to do it?" He looked worried.

"We can...I think. But first we must convince the buying public to try Boniface Olive Oil over their usual brands."

"My family has been growing taggiasca olives for centuries. Their oil is known for its delicate flavor and thick, golden consistency. And I'm sure I can match my competitor's prices."

She nodded. "I've tasted it at every meal, and I don't doubt the quality of your product, or our ability to compete in pricing. But it's the quality I'd like to emphasize. The difference between table wine and champagne." She grabbed a pencil and notepad and scribbled a few words. "I like that...we may use it later."

She flicked off the TV. "This is where imagination enters. What I'd like to do is introduce the American public to your oil and the land of Apulia at the same time." This was the concept that had finally grabbed her and held on through the weeks of planning. She was so excited, she only hoped Antonio would share her enthusiasm.

Maria continued without allowing him time to react to her initial statement. "Virtually no one has heard of this magical place. I want your oil, the *masseria*, castle, town and fields to become inseparable in American minds. When a customer sees a bottle of your oil on a store shelf, she will immediately envision your wild and beautiful rock-strewn groves, this ancestral estate, the streets of Carovigno. Every time she cooks with your oil, it will be like taking a little trip to Italy."

He laughed. "Sounds like a great trick. But how do you propose to pull it off?"

"I've already located a top-notch film crew based in Rome. They're available within a few weeks. They'll record the groves as you harvest, take additional footage of the land and town. We'll emphasize your family tradition of quality and care, starting here and traveling to the customer's kitchen."

She watched Antonio's face for reaction. The bloom of his slow smile told her she was on target. "It sounds good, Maria. Very good. I like it."

"Great! We'll put together a one-minute mélange of scenes that instantly evokes the warm earth, the sun, the smell of ripening olives. But there will be more."

"More scenes?"

"Another angle. Not only will the prospective buyer view this beautiful land and hear it described in coordinated radio advertising, she—or he, as we have many fine male cooks—will have the opportunity to actually visit Carovigno. To compete in our contest, customers simply tell us their favorite use for Boniface Olive Oil. We will choose winners based on originality."

He thought for a long while, his eyes distant. Maria held her breath, wondering if something about this second stage of her proposal had put him off. If he didn't agree to everything she proposed, she had a Plan B as backup. But in her opinion it wouldn't be nearly as effective.

"It all sounds wonderful," he said at last, grabbing her and pulling her in for a big hug. "When do we get started?"

"In two weeks. Using an Italian film crew will give the ads a different flavor from most American ads, and it will be good local PR. But I'll need a translator, if the crew doesn't speak English."

"I have someone in mind. Let me contact her for you. What about a script for the voice-overs?"

He was sharp, very sharp, she thought. "I've been working on a draft. Before we begin shooting I'll have finished it."

He smiled at her. "You're not only lovely, you're brilliant."

Maria stared down at her hands, pleased more than she'd ever admit to him. His praise meant a lot, but her own pride in her work was even more important to her.

More than anything, she wanted to do well—for Antonio and for herself, and the competition was powerful! Her future in the business clearly rested on the success of this project. If she didn't have a future with Antonio, she was determined she'd make a future for herself in other ways that satisfied her.

It was a sunny day in early September when the Italian film crew first congregated in the *masseria's* yard between the main house and the equipment sheds. The filming continued for over a week in the groves, then moved to the mill and factory, and finally shifted to color shots of the countryside around Carovigno. Atmosphere, light, hues were critical to the image Maria wished to convey to her viewers. And although she was no expert in filmmaking, the production team she'd chosen was, and they produced dazzling footage.

The difficult part would come with the editing. From the many hours of film shot, she would have to carve out sixty perfect seconds to represent Boniface Olive Oils.

Throughout these long, arduous days, there was one constant. No matter how challenging, how exhausting the filming for her, or the labor in the fields for Antonio, they stopped work by 8:00 p.m., dined together on his patio, then retreated to their *trullo*. He made love to her each night. Sometimes sweet, gentle, soothing love that melted her bones, leaving her limp and relaxed, free of the day's anxiety. Sometimes fast, hard, hunger-driven love that satisfied the wicked little urges that popped into her mind during the day when she thought of him.

This morning, she watched Antonio approaching through the garden, while she sat over a cup of strong Italian espresso. He had woken before her and left her to sleep a little longer. Wearing a wide-brimmed straw hat, off-white muslin shirt and loose pants of the same material, and tall leather boots, as the fields were muddy that day from rain— he looked the perfect gentleman farmer. At the same time he might have stepped off a page of *GQ*. Hot. Tropical. Set against a wall of fiery red hibiscus, he reminded her of a painting by Gauguin in his Polynesian period.

"Ciao," she said, holding a hand out to him.

"Buongiorno." He lifted her fingertips to his lips and kissed them lightly. "Where is your crew today?"

"On their way back to the factory. I let your foreman know. Hope that's all right."

"It's fine. I had to get out to the fields early. Last night's winds blew away some of the netting beneath the trees. We lost some prime fruit, but at least with the nets back in place again we've minimized the damage."

"I should be off to the factory myself," she admitted with a sigh. "But it's just so lovely out here in the garden, lingering over a cup."

She traced one finger around the lip of the hand-painted demitasse cup, decorated with a proud little rooster, the city symbol of nearby Grottaglie, where it had been made. She would miss this place, these people. Sadness sat heavily on her chest for a moment, an unwelcome distraction from an exciting day.

But before she could stand up to leave, a shriek rose from the little villa on the far side of the garden. Genevra tore between rose bushes, her hands waving frantically above her head, her face contorted in agony.

"Tonio, Tonio—ho perso, Michael!"

Antonio ran to his mother. "You can't have just lost him. Did he wander from the house?" he asked her in Italian.

Maria only caught every third word or so, but it was enough to worry her. It seemed Genevra had awakened that morning and since she didn't hear the child stirring in his room, assumed he was still asleep. When she went in to get him out of his bed, he hadn't been there.

Antonio smiled indulgently. So his little son was an adventurer. He remembered sneaking out of his own bed at a very young age to investigate forbidden nooks and rooms in the *masseria*. "We'll find him," he assured her.

"I'll look in the house," Maria offered, "and ask the maids if they've seen him. He's used to coming to my room. Maybe he saw his *nonna* napping and set out to try and find me."

Genevra cast her a poisonous look. "You have been trying to take him from me all along. Now look what has happened."

Antonio glared at his mother. "This is no time for petty jealousy. Maria has done nothing but help his family. Now let's find the child." He rushed off toward the gate, intending first to alert his men stationed there. They would send up an alarm to the groundskeepers and other employees, who would keep an eye out for the little boy.

Maria watched Antonio go then turned to Genevra to offer a comforting word. But the woman merely turned and stalked away.

Maria searched all the places that might appeal to a little boy. But found no trace of him.

After two hours had passed, Antonio sent men into the nearby fields to search, even though it seemed impossible for Michael to have slipped past the gate guards. Genevra looked stricken, her hands shaking as she left the wrought-iron bench in the garden where she'd waited for word. She moved unsteadily toward her villa.

Maria sighed. Somehow she had to make peace with the

woman. She might not like Genevra very much but, in a
way, she did understand her. The child's grandmother probably didn't want to be blamed for his having gone missing.
And so she had picked on Maria as a convenient scapegoat.

Maria found her sitting on the stone stoop leading up to
her front door. The woman's cheeks were cuttlebone white.
Her hands, clenched in her lap, showed blue at the knuck-
les.

Maria silently sat down beside her, put an arm around
her shoulders. "They'll find him. Let me take you inside
and make you a cup of tea."

Genevra slowly turned her head to observe her. Deep
lines had been etched across her forehead, around her
mouth by the Italian sun. Her eyes were the color of the
earth of Carovigno, her hair streaked with white.

Tradition plays an important role here, Maria thought.
Grandparents are venerated. Maybe, in a way, she had unintentionally disturbed a delicate familial balance.

Taking Genevra's hand, she coaxed her off the stoop and
led her into the house. Maria helped her sit on a hard
wooden chair before the kitchen table. Finding a teakettle
on the stove, she filled it with water and lit a burner. Cups
and saucers, loose tea leaves and honey were in the cupboard. She arranged all on the table while Antonio's mother
sat in grim silence.

"Are you cold?" Maria asked, noting how she had
wrapped her arms around herself.

Genevra seemed not to have heard her question. "What
will happen to *mio bambino*—out there alone?"

Maria touched her shoulder. "They'll find him." She
wished she could believe, without a moment's doubt, that
was true. For now, all she could do was hope.

She went in search of Genevra's shawl, the black wool
knitted one she often wore on chill mornings. But it wasn't
in her bedroom. Neither had Maria seen it lying about in
the living room. From the hallway, she spotted something

draped over the back of the rocking chair in Michael's room.

She was about to snatch the knitted square off the chair when she saw the piece of paper pinned to it. Stepping closer, she read words scrawled in black ink.

Her heart faltered. She gasped. "Dear God, no!"

Thirteen

The *polizia* had come and gone. They had searched all the *masseria* and the surrounding fields, although Antonio's men had already combed them for hours, looking for the little boy.

Fingerprints had been taken from Michael's room. Photographs of Michael had been handed over. The ransom note was to be analyzed by an expert flying down from Rome.

No one made any promises. Kidnappings in Italy, customarily, did not end well. Victims often were never seen again. Not alive.

Everyone knew it, but no one said it.

"I can't do this!" Antonio growled as he paced his office that afternoon. "There must be something we can—" His voice cracked.

Maria touched his arm, her heart aching for the man, for his son. "The police will let us know as soon as they hear anything. You'll leave the money, as requested, in the piazza in Brindisi, in two days. That's all you *can* do.''

"Money!" He swore in Italian. "This is Marco's doing. I can taste it. If I ever get my hands on the idiot I'll kill him."

"Antonio," she said soothingly, "we have no proof it's him. The captain said it could be anyone. You admitted to him that you have enemies."

"Competition—not enemies! There's a difference." He shook his head savagely.

The police had brought up the possibility of someone holding a grudge against *Il Principe* or his family, but the only person he could think of was Marco. He'd continued to have the Serilo brothers followed. His men had sworn the young men were at home all the previous night, but when the police went to speak with them, Frederico's wife couldn't tell them where her husband and brother-in-law were.

The police had also suggested a possible connection with terrorists. And at those words, Antonio had seen a mixture of horror and denial flash across Maria's face. Emotions he shared with her. But it wouldn't be the first time that the child of the wealthy Italian was kidnapped for ransom, hoping to raise money for weapons.

"I don't know what to think...or do." Antonio stopped in front of the casement windows overlooking the garden and stared, jaw locked, fists clenched in helpless protest at his sides. "Terrorists...it just doesn't feel right," he growled. "The ransom note asked for enough money to make a poor man feel lucky. Not enough to fund an army."

He whipped around, pulled her into his arms and held her, needing an anchor, something or someone to cling to when his world seemed to be slipping away from him. "Stay here." His lips moved against the fine strands of hair on top of her head. "I'm going to look for that bastard and my son."

"But where will you search that the police haven't?" she protested.

"Anywhere Marco might think to go. Anywhere he might feel safe."

After he left, Maria closed her eyes and concentrated on breathing. Inside, she was dying. Poor little Michael. He must be so very frightened. She prayed the kidnappers, whoever they were, hadn't hurt him.

Two of the youngest housemaids stepped into the room, their eyes red from weeping. "Is there anything we can do, *signorina?*" one asked.

"No. Just see to your mistress. The doctor says the sedatives may wear off soon. When they do, she should take another pill. Try to keep her calm." Genevra's physician had voiced concern over her heart. The shock of her grandson's kidnapping had shaken the woman badly. Her blood pressure had skyrocketed.

For another three hours, Maria sat and waited helplessly. The sun had reached its golden zenith hours before and was now sinking relentlessly toward the western horizon. In a few more hours, it would be dark. Effective searching would become impossible.

Her chest hurt as if her heart had been torn from it. Her head had been aching for hours. She might feel better if she lay down, but didn't have the strength or will to go to her room.

If Antonio was right and Marco was behind the kidnapping of the child, perhaps the final outcome still had a chance of being a happy one. She was unconvinced, from the little she'd seen of him at the market, that he was capable of killing.

If only she knew how to help, even in the smallest way...

It was nearly midnight when Antonio returned to the villa. Maria had been watching for him from the garden, lit by torches. His face was drained of all color. Caverns of gray smudged the flesh beneath his eyes. He looked as if the last ounce of strength had been sucked from his body.

"Mio cara," he gasped, falling into her arms.

She held him in silence, asking no questions, simply offering comfort. At last she whispered, "Come, you must rest."

He pulled away from her and stared fiercely across the fields. His shoulders shuddered, but the rest he kept in. The conqueror, defeated.

"I can't. There must be somewhere I haven't looked."

"I'm sure that anywhere you haven't searched, the police have. You won't do Michael any good driving yourself this way." She stroked the line of his chin. How very fragile he looked now. She loved him all the more for his vulnerability. "Come to bed. Just for an hour or two. With a little rest you'll be able to think more clearly."

He didn't respond to her, but let her pull him toward the stairs that led to his bedroom. Once inside, she closed the door behind them. Maria turned on only the lamp closest to the bed. It cast pale shadows across the room. In the near dark, Antonio looked even more gaunt.

He sat, woodenly, on the bed. She knelt down, untied his shoes and removed first them then his socks

Standing up before him she unbuttoned his shirt. Tenderly, she eased the soft muslin fabric off his shoulders and down his arms. Beneath his clothing, muscles shaped a strong body, but Antonio looked anything but strong now. He was a broken man. A man without enough will to function on the simplest level.

She unbuckled his pants, loosened the waistband, then gently pressed her palm to his bare chest, easing him back onto the bed, his head onto the pillow. When she brought the sheet up over him, he reached out and seized her wrist.

"Lie with me, *cara.* Hold me, please," he whispered hoarsely, urgently.

Maria toed off her shoes, stepped from her dress, then

slipped beneath the sheet in her underwear. Stretching out alongside his taut body, she rested her head on his shoulder, smoothed a hand soothingly across his bare chest.

She wished with all her heart that she had the power to make everything right again. The magic to bring his son safely back to him. She could guess his thoughts, the punishing doubts assaulting him. He blamed himself for not keeping a closer watch on the child. Perhaps he had been neglectful as a parent in some respects, but it hadn't been intentional. He loved Michael.

After what seemed a long time, his breathing slowed, deepened. She thought he might have fallen asleep, but when she tried to change her position, his arms tightened around her like the powerful wires that staked out his olive trees. "Please. Don't leave yet," he whispered.

His words were as precious as jewels. She was important to him, even during these terrible times.

She could think of only one way to take his mind off of Michael, to ease him toward rest. Slowly, she began moving her hand in soothing spirals across his chest, caressing the ridges and mounds, stroking away the awful tension. She could feel muscles start to unknot. Sensed when the tendons in his throat lengthened, allowing his head to roll to one side against the pillow. She looked up to see his lips part on a silent sigh.

"Now doesn't seem the time," he murmured regretfully.

"Now is the perfect time," she said. "We need each other."

"I'm not sure how much you need me, Maria," he choked out the words. "But I've never needed you more."

She slipped off her bra and panties, pushing them out from beneath the sheet and onto the floor. Antonio lay unmoving, watching her solemnly. She rolled over on top of him, let her body melt into his. Her breasts pressed into the curls of fur across his chest. Her hips angled against the firm plane of his stomach. She felt him harden, lengthen against her thighs. Corded flesh against her silk. Her body responded instantly, although he hadn't touched her.

"Rest," she whispered. "Let me."

He looked up at her, his eyes brimming with emotion. He rested his hands on her hips as she sat up, swung a leg over his hips, centered herself over him. Settling over him, she allowed her body's weight to drive her down as he lifted his hips to move deeper within her.

Antonio let out a shuddering, primal moan. "Woman...ah! *Mi piace.*"

With each feminine thrust, she felt a little of the paralyzing tension and exhaustion leave him. Then he was crying out her name, again and again, his body shuddering fiercely. And he raked his wide fingers through her hair, pulled her down onto his chest and held her there, his mouth on hers, their bodies locked in timeless union.

And when it was over he slept.

Maria turned over in bed and let her arm fall away to the other side of the mattress. The side Antonio had occupied. She felt only bedding.

Perhaps there had been news of Michael?

She launched herself from the bed. Dressed quickly, descended to the kitchen where Sophia was feeding both the household and grounds staff, as well as four armed police officers. With disappointment she noted that Antonio wasn't in the group. The uniformed men stood up from the long trencher table when she entered.

"What has happened?" she asked the man who had seemed in charge the day before.

He shook his head sadly. "We still have men going door to door through Carovigno and the neighboring towns." He spoke slowly in Italian, so that she was able to understand. "Others combing the countryside. Our fear, *signorina*, is that the kidnappers may have moved the child out of the immediate area. Safer for them. All it would take is for one of them to remain behind and pick up the ransom.''

Maria shivered at the thought of Michael being spirited farther away from his home by strangers.

She turned to Angela. ''Where is La Signora?''

''I took her breakfast tray, but she doesn't eat, Miss Maria.'' The young woman frowned. ''*Il dottore,* he says she is better off sleeping. He came and gave her an injection when she wouldn't take her pills.''

Maria nodded. The doctor was a wise man. In many ways she'd have preferred to sleep through the next day or two. At least, so long as there was nothing she could do.

But if she could help…

''Does anyone know where Antonio is?'' she asked, looking around the table. The four officers had taken their seats again and were hurriedly finishing their breakfast.

''*Il Principe,* he was in the garden an hour ago,'' one of the groundsmen offered.

''I saw him leave by the back gate twenty minutes ago,'' the young houseboy volunteered.

Maria politely turned down the cook's offer of a warm breakfast. She had no appetite at all. Walking outside, she looked around the yard and garden, but Antonio wasn't there. His sleek, black car was sitting in the courtyard, though, key in its ignition.

By late afternoon, he still hadn't returned, and there was no word of where he might be. No news of Michael either. She was nearly out of her mind with worry. The police told her all that could be done now was to wait and see if Michael was returned when the ransom was paid the next day, as arranged. They didn't look happy with the situation.

She'd never felt more frightened in her life.

On impulse Maria flung herself into the driver's seat of the Ferrari, turned the key and drove to the gate. ''I'll be back before dark,'' she told the guard, and he let her out with a solemn salute.

As Maria drove, she thought about the places Antonio had taken her since her arrival in Italy. Where, among them, might a kidnapper successfully hide a young child if not in a house nearby?

There were fishing villages all up and down the coast. If this was Marco's doing, it was possible that he had taken Michael away by boat. Was even now hiding him offshore, but she knew his resources were limited. How could he afford a boat unless he stole it?

Then there was the beach she'd visited that one day, near Specchiola. She couldn't recall how far it was, but it had taken only ten minutes to drive there, and it had been straight down the coastal road, so it shouldn't be difficult to find. Hadn't Antonio said he'd played on the cliffs, in the caves there as a boy? He had guessed at that time that other children had also, still did. Marco had come to this beach too, with his brother, to pick up women. Antonio's men had followed them there. It was worth checking out, she decided as she drove the Ferrari along the twisting shore road. A ribbon of chalk-white sand edged aquamarine surf. So, where would Marco take Michael? Where would he feel safe? Where no one would be likely to search for him until he had cash in hand.

Her heart beating faster, Maria pulled the car with a screech off the highway and onto a local road that soon became unpaved.

Caves, she thought. Caves that wind through limestone cliffs are wonderful hiding places.

Parking the car, she walked between little pastel villas bordering the beach. She stopped to ask several women in the street if they'd seen either of the Serilos, or a little boy…and she described Michael. But they all shook their heads.

She continued on across the sand. The fishing dories were out, only a few nets remained, having been hung out to dry. An old man sat on a rock, mending a net by hand, watching the water, working automatically as if he could see through the tips of his fingers. As she came closer she noticed that his eyes were cloudy, and she guessed he was mostly blind. Yet his stitches were exact and strong.

She stopped beside him. "Did a little boy come this way with two men?" she asked. He might have heard them even if he couldn't see.

The old man straightened up but didn't answer.

She tried in her broken Italian. *"Un bambino e due uomi...dove?"* It was the best she could do with her nerves singing in her ears.

His eyes widened, although they remained unfocused. *"Si."* He continued in Italian, and she thought she understood...something about early one morning, before his sons left to fish.

"Dove?" she asked excitedly.

He pointed down the beach. *That way!*

Her heart raced as her gaze followed the direction of his finger. At the far end of the beach were a few houses, but before them were the low cliffs...and the caves.

Maria hesitated only a moment. *"Molte grazie,"* she murmured, patting the old man's hands as she started to move away from him then broke into a run.

She jogged along the beach, then cut up across the sand to the base of the cliffs where she imagined she'd be less likely to be seen. She considered driving back to the villa to tell the police that she knew where Michael was, but it seemed premature.

She kicked herself for not taking the time to bring her cell phone with her. Then she might have simply called the *masseria* and alerted the police to the possibility. She also could have checked to see if Antonio had returned.

Maria was glad she had worn her good, rubber-soled walking shoes instead of sandals. The limestone ledges, encrusted with barnacles, were sharp and might have sliced through thin leather soles. She had to be careful how she

KATHRYN JENSEN   171

gripped the rocks above her. By the time she reached the
mouth of the first cave, her palms were raw. She wiped
traces of blood on her shorts and peered into the darkness,
listening.

Nothing.

Maria moved further along the ledge, then up to the next
higher cave. When she reached it, she thought it was as
empty sounding as the first, and was about to move on to
another when she heard a soft snuffling sound.

She backed up. Listened harder.

A man's voice shouted, *"Silencio!"*

The crying only increased. She cautiously peered around
the edge of rock, into the opening of the cave. A lantern's
glow shimmered against the inside walls.

Slowly, she moved closer, until she could see a crude
pallet spread with a blanket. On it lay Michael, one little
ankle chained to a rusty anchor. He kicked his foot, wailed
and threw himself down on the dirty blanket, then pulled
at the chain with his hands, continuing to wail.

Her heart broke.

"I said, keep your trap shut!" a voice yelled in a rough
Italian dialect.

She shifted her line of sight, and there was Marco, his
brother sitting on the floor of the cave beside him.

"He's too young to understand," Frederico said. "He's
scared. I told you we shouldn't do this."

"It's working. They have my demands. All we have to
do is pick up the money tomorrow morning. You think a
Boniface isn't going to pay for his own blood? His only
son?" He laughed nastily. "We should have asked for
twice as much. He would have paid." Marco turned back
to Michael, whose wails had merged into a single ear-
piercing screech. "Shut up or I'll put the gag back on you,
kid."

Maria had no trouble understanding what was going on.
And she could read the fear in the little boy's eyes.

She wished she had some kind of weapon. A gun!

She'd drive off the two men and take Michael away. As it was, she had no means of forcing them to give up the child. Maybe they were armed anyway! And she knew nothing about guns and starting a shooting match would be foolish, only put the child and herself in worse danger.

Her only alternative was to go for help, but she couldn't bear the thought of leaving Michael with these two desperate men. One more yowl from the child might set off Marco. She wouldn't put it beyond the bastard to strike him.

It would be dark soon.

She wondered if she should wait a while, keeping watch to make sure Michael wasn't harmed. Then, when it was dark, she could sneak in and steal him back while the two men slept.

Maria found a niche just inside the cave's mouth where she would be out of sight. The light began to fade outside, and Michael sobbed more softly, as if too exhausted to produce any volume.

She waited.

At last, the little boy fell asleep, then Frederico nodded off, and last of all Marco. She wore no watch but estimated, after what seemed like a long time, that it must be after midnight. She was stiff and cold from pressing herself into the rock crevice.

Carefully, she inched out from her hiding place. Moving soundlessly across the cave floor, she watched the two men for any sign of consciousness, but neither moved or altered his breathing. She was nearly to Michael, already calculating how she might gently ease him into her arms as she had many times before without waking him, when a squeal of delight erupted through the cave.

"'Ria! 'Ria!"

She stared in horror at the child, pressing a finger to her lips as she spun, looking for a place to hide. Nothing. And there was no time to grab him and make her escape. When she swung around again, Marco Serilo was between her and the cave's entrance, and his brother was sitting up, scowling at her.

Marco grinned demonically. "Hey, brother! Looks like we have a complication."

Fourteen

Antonio had spent the entire day after leaving Maria in bed, in the heat, scouring the countryside on foot. Searching scores of tiny houses, *trulli,* barns and shacks tucked into rocky landscape he thought the police might have missed. He returned exhausted, defeated, to the main house in the early morning hours.

He didn't go upstairs to the bedroom. He wouldn't disturb Maria, didn't wish to talk about the discouraging day. The police, when he'd contacted them during the day and night, had had no better luck, and now they were talking about the possibility that Michael might have been taken out of the country.

For the first time in his life he understood the anguish of a young mother who loses her child. As a father robbed of his son, he felt no less pain. He felt utterly helpless.

Antonio poured himself a grappa from the crystal carafe in his office. The strong, thick liquor burned its way down his throat, simmered in his belly. He had never cared for the taste of the stuff. Tonight it seemed mild punishment for his failure as a father. He vowed if Michael was brought home safely, things would change. *He* would change. He would be more of a father to the little boy.

More of a man in other ways too.

Antonio sank onto the couch, buried his face in his hands. He couldn't have said when the tears stopped and his body sagged limply against the cushions.

He woke with a start and looked around the dark room. Through the window streamed a faint peach-colored light, the shade of the inside of a seashell, and he knew dawn wasn't far away. He forced himself to his feet and wearily climbed the stairs, wanting to stop in and see that Maria was all right before he splashed water on his face and went off again to meet with the police captain who would oversee the payment of the ransom.

As soon as he walked through the bedroom door, he sensed that something was wrong. One look at the bed assured him this was so. It hadn't been slept in. After a quick search of the house and grounds, he realized that Maria was no longer on the property and his car was missing.

No one else in the household would have borrowed it. Maria. Had she gone after Michael?

Panic consuming him, he ran for the gate. "The American woman...have you seen her?"

The guard checked his log. "She left last evening in your car, Your Highness. I just came on duty, but it doesn't look as if she's come back yet."

His mind whirled, then stuck on first hopeful, then horrifying possibilities. If she'd somehow found Michael...wouldn't that be wonderful! But then why wasn't she back here? What had happened to keep her from returning?

The only answer he could come up with set him reeling. *Someone had stopped her!*

For a long moment, he couldn't move. The fear of losing

both of them was devastating. He struggled to think. Calmly, rationally. But in the end he did what he'd always done, what had always worked when he was troubled or confused.

He gazed out across the fields at the gnarled, ancient olive trees ranging away from the villa. The instincts that his ancestors had taken into battle, had won them the land he now cultivated, had brought victory over invaders and the elements, surged into action.

It was morning.

Maria watched the light alter almost imperceptibly from nonexistent to a dim, pearly gray, to the clear blue-white of the earliest hours of day. Little Michael lay with his head in her lap. As soon as Marco had seen the calming effect Maria had on the little boy, he'd put the two of them together and lashed only Maria to the anchor.

She hadn't slept, but Michael had snuggled up in her lap and closed his eyes as soon as she'd started singing softly to him. She hadn't dared sleep for fear of what the two men might do to her. Or to the child.

They were still arguing while she pretended to sleep.

"I say we take them down to the beach and let them go." Frederico stood up from the rock where he had been sitting and stood over his brother. "If we tell no one where they are, it is as good as murder. They will starve to death, if the cold doesn't get them first."

"So it is a different form of punishment for *Il Principe* than I'd planned. It is no less effective," Marco sneered. "Probably better. He has so much money, giving us a little wouldn't hurt him. This—" he waved a hand toward his captives "—this will hurt him very deeply. It is appropriate."

Maria's heart pounded wildly within her chest. Her eyes burned but remained dry. She would never see Antonio again. She would never be able to tell him how much she loved him, how precious his little boy was to her, how desperately she had come to love this magnificent country of his. All of that was impossible now.

But most of all, she mourned little Michael's fate. If there was anything she could do to give him a chance of surviving …

"You don't want to do that!" she blurted out, her heart shooting up into her throat.

The two men spun and glared at her.

"Do what? Kill you?" Marco laughed low and meanly in his throat. "But you've spoiled everything, *signorina.* You've left us no choice. Don't insult me by claiming you wouldn't identify us if we released you."

"Of course I'd turn you in," she snapped at him. "Without hesitation. But the baby. He's innocent. Your brother is right. No court in the world would take the statement of a three-year-old as proof of identity. And he's still worth as much to you as before, perhaps more. If you return him safely to his father."

In Frederico's sad gaze she saw compassion and respect. He knew she was begging for the child's life. "She's right, Marco. Leave her here. We will take the child and get the money coming to us."

"No!" Marco roared, suddenly wild with rage. "The money isn't enough! She is just an employee to him. She means nothing to *Il Principe.* But the child. If he is never found, the man will suffer all of his life. I have decided." He pounded a fist to his own chest. "It is what I want."

"But it's not what I want!" a voice echoed from the mouth of the cave.

Marco nearly fell over as he swung about to face a different Antonio Boniface than Maria had ever seen. Silhouetted against the sunshine-filled opening of the cave, his dark figure nearly filled the space. His eyes were deep, blue-black pits of reckoning. The set of his mouth was vicious. His voice barely contained his fury.

"Don't come any closer," Marco snarled. "I have your son and the *signorina*. Both will die before you take me."

"I don't think so, Marco."

Marco grinned and pulled a gun from beneath his shirt. "*I* think so."

"No, Marco!" Frederico pleaded. "It has gone too far. A little money was all right, but this is murder." He reached for his brother's gun, but Marco snatched it away from him.

"If you want to punish anyone, make it me, Marco," Antonio growled, taking a step closer to the man. "Kill me. That's what you really want to do. Isn't it?"

"No!" Maria cried, clutching Michael to her. The child woke with a start and began to cry.

Antonio ignored them. "I'm going to take that gun away from you, Marco. Then I'm going to take my child and my woman home. You aren't going to hurt anyone."

Marco frowned at Antonio, his mouth quirking into a quizzical grimace, as if he didn't understand what was happening. "You fool. I am the one with the gun!

He raised the muzzle toward Antonio's chest.

Maria screamed, crushing Michael's head to her breast, covering both his eyes and ears. In the back of her mind Antonio's words reverberated: *My woman…my woman…my woman.* But it's too late, a voice warned. Too late!

Suddenly, one thing after another happened so quickly she could barely follow the motions.

With a shout of anguish, Frederico threw himself at his brother, missing the gun. The weapon fired, and Antonio tackled Marco, landing on top of him on the floor of the cave. Then, from the shadows behind Maria came a strange scurrying noise, scrambling footfalls, shouts, an explosion of men in uniform.

In seconds, the nightmare was over.

The police, arriving through a connecting tunnel to the cave, had cuffed Marco and his brother, escorted them out of the cave and down to the beach where official vehicles waited.

Antonio cradled Michael in his arms, pulled Maria to his chest as she closed his eyes with blessed relief. He brushed the top of her head with his lips and whispered over and over into the pale wisps of hair, "Thank you. Thank you for finding my son, Maria."

She nodded against his shirt, soaked with her own tears. Swallowed the salty flow, trying to stop crying, wanting to speak but still unable.

"Are you all right?" he asked. "They didn't hurt you?"

"No, I'm fine. Michael is too. I've already checked him out. He was giving them one hell of a list of complaints. Just like his father. Won't take anything from anyone."

Antonio smiled dimly and kissed her forehead for good measure as they walked from the cave.

"How did you find us?" she asked.

"We saw the Ferrari on the road. The caves echo even soft voices. We heard loud arguing and followed the sounds. Now let's go home."

She dug in her heels and looked up at him, at last blinking away tears. "Just one thing."

"Yes?"

"*Your woman?*" She pursed her lips and waited.

He rolled his eyes. "I guessed you'd want an explanation for that."

But it was two days later before that conversation would be completed. During that time, the press was constantly at the gates and calling on the phone. The Serilo brothers had been arraigned in court in Brindisi, and were being held for trial.

In addition, Antonio had flown hastily to Rome then to Naples for reasons unclear to Maria. All she knew was that he'd assured her the trips were important and had to do with the groves.

While he was gone, she spent time with Michael and, to her surprise, Genevra. Antonio's mother asked her to dinner one day, to lunch the next, and the woman had been remarkably civil. She never directly thanked Maria for her role in rescuing her grandchild, but it seemed a foregone conclusion that relations between the two women would be different from here on.

It was all the thanks Maria needed.

The rest of her days were full of last-minute details related to the advertising campaign. There was still a great deal to do if they were to launch Boniface Olive Oil before the holiday season, but most of the work could be handled in the States.

Maria was both excited and saddened by the prospect of seeing her plans come to fruition. The completion of her job meant the end of her days in Italy, with Antonio.

On the evening he returned from Rome, Antonio asked Maria to dine with him in his suite. Hours earlier, he had seemed preoccupied and solemn. She feared that the trauma of the last few days had reinstated his fear of loss. Her heart ached at the thought of their parting.

Maria dressed with care for their dinner. One of their last, it seemed. She chose one of her favorite dresses—dazzling white cotton, full-skirted with an off-the-shoulder neckline and cap sleeves. She had bought it at *mercato* one sunny morning. It would always remind her of Italy.

The night was warm and fragrant with lushly blooming roses in the garden. Antonio had arranged for their meal to be served on a table on the patio outside his rooms. Candles in cut-glass globes lined the surrounding low stone wall. Flowers adorned the table. The setting was decidedly romantic, and if she hadn't been so nervous she would have been entranced by his thoughtfulness.

When Maria finally sat down, he held out a stem of crystal-white wine to her. "At last we have time to relax in privacy."

"Yes," she agreed, sipping, letting liquid silver course sweetly down her throat, feeling not at all relaxed. "To say we've both been busy lately would be a ridiculous understatement."

"I've noticed you've done a lot in just two days to move our project along," he commented.

"You read my report?" She had left it on his desk for his return, but hadn't thought he'd had time to even glance at it.

"Yes. It's brilliant. All of it, Maria. Such a strategist—you ought to have been a general."

She laughed and set her glass down. "I don't know about that. I just think this is an approach that will work well with American buyers. And we were very fortunate with the filming." She drew a satisfied breath and let it out. "We're going to have a very effective TV commercial."

She paused. But when he didn't pick up the conversation and the moment threatened to turn awkward, she prompted him. "And you've been traveling..."

He nodded. "My lawyer is in Rome. And I ship out of Naples, through a branch of my family. I needed to speak to people in both places because I'm considering some important changes in—" He hesitated.

"In the company's structure?" she guessed. "Because you'll now be exporting to a new market?"

"Changes that affect the company, yes, but also my personal life. I had to get a realistic sense of the impact they would have." He looked at her, hard. As if trying to see through to her core, to her soul.

She frowned. His serious tone and that steely gaze focused on her suggested that she had something to do with all of this.

"Maybe you'd better explain," she murmured.

He stood up from the table, pulled his chair around to

sit beside her and took her hand between his two. "I want you to forget everything I've said in the past."

"Everything?" she asked, more confused than ever.

"I told you once I would never marry again. I meant it…then. I didn't know you'd play such a critical role in my life. In my son's life. Maria, you seem to be taking this all very casually. But *I* know what you did. You saved my son's life."

She lowered her head. So that's what this is all about, she thought a little sadly. A thank-you dinner. She was grateful that Antonio appreciated her. But it was a bitter-sweet end to their romance.

Then she looked up from her lap and saw the ring resting in the center of his palm.

"Oh!"

"It's not your style. Far too large for your small hand. Too ornate for today's styles. But I would be proud if you'd wear it."

The diamond was enormous. Probably five carats. Encircling it was a generous row of rubies as red as royal blood. The band and rich encrusting around the stones had the look of antiquity, yet the gold shone as if it had been cast that day, just for her.

"It's unbelievable," she sighed, overwhelmed at so generous a gift.

"It has been the engagement ring of the Boniface for over three hundred years. Our brides have worn it until they were ready to pass it along to a son or daughter."

"Brides?" she asked, staring up at him, feeling muddled, desperate for words she could cling to that made sense, and more than a little dizzy. "Antonio, you're talking in riddles. Please, don't make me think this is something other than a reward for Michael."

He groaned and smiled down at her apologetically. "I'm sorry. I'm doing this all wrong. It's difficult…I just don't want to lose you, *cara.* I want you to marry me. Please marry me.''

He was down on one knee, she suddenly realized. The man was kneeling before her! Kneeling! And saying those beautiful, impossible, wondrous words!

"Say it again."

He laughed. "You don't believe me?"

"I don't believe I'm hearing it. *Say it!*"

"I love you, Maria. Marry me...please! I've spent the last two days making sure that my lawyers, my employees, my mother and everyone else understands that you are going to be my wife and play an active role in this company. We Italians love politics, and the family—both by blood and by profession—had to be prepared for such a change. Now that they are, I can promise you everything you deserve. I know your career is important to you. As my wife, you will also be CEO in charge of worldwide marketing.''

A husband. A professional future so amazing she could only have imagined it in a dream. And a family?

"What about children?" The words tumbled out on top of each other. She watched his expression. "I'll always love Michael as my own, but..."

"I know," he admitted. "I said that too, didn't I?"

"You said, no more children."

"If I can risk taking you as my wife...I can take any risk. I do want more children. And this time I will raise them in partnership with their mother.''

It was all falling into place. Love felt as if it was swelling to fill all the gaps in her life with rich and satisfying details beyond anything she could have hoped for. But there still remained one knotty issue...

"What about *Nonna? Genevra?*"

Antonio winced. "She has been difficult, hasn't she? I expect Michael will always be special to her, but she and I had a serious discussion before I left for Rome. My mother understands that she will have our respect and love, as long as she lets us raise our children without interference and returns that respect. I told her you would never try to force her out of her home, or keep her grandchildren from her.''

''That's true,'' she agreed immediately.

''I also bribed her.''

''You didn't.''

''I told her you would give her many, many *bambini* to cuddle.''

Maria laughed. ''Now that was wicked of you.''

He winked at her and squeezed her hand. ''Not really. I intend to deliver.''

That night Maria slept in Antonio's bed in the main house with his ring on her finger. And they began to create a new generation of Bonifaces. A family who would struggle and love, and sweat over the soil that had been theirs for centuries untold. A family whose dedication to the land and devotion to each other would coax from the earth its savory fruit and continue their proud heritage.

Epilogue

The central office of Klein & Klein Public Relations and Advertising, in Washington, D.C., on Connecticut Avenue shifted into high gear. Although their client list included many important names from politics, industry and the entertainment business, they were always hungry for a big, new name. And Boniface Olive Oil, which had been unknown in the U.S. only a year before, was now one of the fastest growing importers of its kind.

Tamara Jackson was flying high that morning. She lived for challenges. Prided herself on being better than good at her job. She'd won her share of high-powered clients for the company. But none so distinguished as Boniface Olive Oil. She was good at playing it cool, but inside nerves clandestinely prickled at her.

Tamara tapped lightly on the conference room door and strode through without waiting for an answer. On the far side of the room a woman, elegant in black silk, stood gazing out the windows. She wore a hat—very chic, retro-forties—the short, bead-flecked veil shadowing the upper part of her face. Just enough to add allure. Her blond hair was swept up beneath it in a sophisticated coif.

Tamara envied her immediately. "La Principessa, welcome to Washington. I hope your flight was comfortable."

"It was just fine," the woman said, turning to face her.

Tamara fell back a step. The woman's English was flawless.

Unaccented. No, that wasn't quite right. There was an American edge to it. She frowned, took closer note of the features behind the semi-sheer veiling.

"You're American."

"*Si.*" The woman said, reaching up to remove the diamond stickpin from her hat and the hat from her head. "Hello, Tamara. How have you been?"

"Maria!?" She swallowed, fell back a step. Sat down on whatever it was that had just struck the back of her knees. "Ohmygod! It's…how did?"

"Are you all right?" Maria asked, sounding genuinely concerned.

"Am I all right?" Tamara gasped. "I had no idea. I…my word, look at you, girl…I mean. I'm sorry, *Principessa*…Maria… Do I call you Your Highness?" She was babbling, nearly incoherent. Pull it together, Tam, she told herself ruthlessly. "You sure gave me a jolt."

Maria smiled sweetly at her. "I intended to." Her smile faded.

Then Tamara got it.

"All the times we tormented you. I'm so sorry. I suppose we just got carried away. You were such an easy target."

"I suppose I was."

The emphasis on the final word. Yes, Tamara thought, I'll bet you've grown up a great deal since leaving Klein & Klein. The change was unbelievable.

Tamara bit down on her bottom lip, took a deep breath, accepted the inevitable.

"This beats all of our little tricks," she admitted. "Just look at you. Well, I suppose there's no point in our continuing this meeting." She tapped two crimson lacquered fingernails on the thick proposal file she'd labored so hard to finish on schedule. "Did you just stop by to rub my nose in it? No matter. Who are you contracting with for your advertising? The Masters Agency? Or will it be Zandewski?"

Maria studied her old foe...or the woman she'd believed had been her enemy at one time. She smiled, remembering the pranks played at her expense. Silly things, really. All in good fun. She'd just been too shy to appreciate the camaraderie behind them, to join in the fun instead of running from it.

But now she'd given back as good as she'd gotten. Better even. Delicious.

"I want the best representation possible for Boniface Olive Oil," she said carefully. "And I know from working with you that you've always done a spectacular job for your accounts, Tamara." She sat down at the table, reached over and pulled the file toward her, opened it. "Let's see what you have for me."

Tamara swallowed, smiled, then shoved her own chair closer to the table. Maria hadn't said yes, but she hadn't said no either. "You did the breakout ads, didn't you?"

Maria nodded.

"Awesome!" Tamara beamed, her confidence returning when Maria smiled back. "We're going to make an amazing team, *Principessa*."

*   *   *   *   *

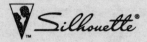

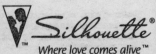

COMING NEXT MONTH

#1501 TAMING THE BEASTLY MD—Elizabeth Bevarly
Dynasties: The Barones
When nurse Rita Barone needed a date for a party, she asked the very
intriguing Dr. Matthew Grayson. Things heated up, and Rita wound up
in Matthew's bed, where he introduced her to sensual delight. However
next morning they vowed to forget their night of passion. But Rita coul
forget. Could she convince the good doctor she needed his loving touch
forever?

#1502 INSTINCTIVE MALE—Cait London
Heartbreakers
Desperate for help, Ellie Lathrop turned to the one man who'd always
gotten under her skin—enigmatic Mikhail Stepanov. Mikhail ignited E
long-hidden desires, and soon she surrendered to their powerful attracti
But proud Mikhail wouldn't accept less than her whole heart, and Ellie
didn't know if she could give him that.

#1503 A BACHELOR AND A BABY—Marie Ferrarella
The Mom Squad
Because of a misunderstanding, Rick Masters had lost Joanna Prescott,
love of his life. But eight years later, Rick drove past Joanna's house—
in time to save her from a fire and deliver her baby. The old chemistry
still there, and Rick fell head over heels for Joanna and her baby. But
Joanna feared being hurt again; could Rick prove his love was rock soli

#1504 TYCOON FOR AUCTION—Katherine Garbera
When Corrine Martin won sexy businessman Rand Pearson at a bachel
auction, she decided he would make the perfect corporate boyfriend. Th
arrangement consisted of three dates. But Corrine found pleasure and
comfort in Rand's embrace, and she found herself in unanticipated
danger—of surrendering to love!

#1505 BILLIONAIRE BOSS—Meagan McKinney
Matched in Montana
He had hired her to be his assistant, but when wealthy Seth Morgan car
face-to-face with beguiling beauty Kirsten Meadows, he knew he wante
be more than just her boss. Soon he was fighting to persuade wary Kirs
to yield to him—one sizzling kiss at a time!

#1506 WARRIOR IN HER BED—Cathleen Galitz
Annie Wainwright had gone to Wyoming seeking healing, not romance.
Then Johnny Lonebear stormed into her life, refusing to be ignored.
Throwing caution to the wind, Annie embarked on a summer fling with
Johnny that grew into something much deeper. But what would happen
once Johnny learned she was carrying his child?